A Voice From
The River

A Voice From
The River

A novel by Dan Gerber

Michigan State University Press
East Lansing

♾ The paper used in this publication meets the minimum requirements
of ANSI/NISO Z39.48-1992 (R 1997) (Permanence of Paper).

Michigan State University Press
East Lansing, Michigan 48823-5245

Printed and bound in the United States of America.

Previously published by Clark City Press 0-944439-20-9
Michigan State University Press Edition 0-87013-755-7

LC Control number 89082472

Cover design by Erin Kirk New
Cover art is pencil, charcoal, and watercolor by Steven Graber
titled *Barfleur* and is used courtesy of the artist.
Author photograph is by Robert Turney.

Michigan State University Press is a member of the Green Press Initiative and
is committed to developing and encouraging ecologically responsible publishing practices. For more information about the Green Press Initiative and the
use of recycled paper in book publishing, please visit *www.greenpressinitiative.org.*

Visit Michigan State University Press on the World Wide Web at
www.msupress.msu.edu

FOR VIRGINIA

Flowering and fading come to us both at once.
And somewhere lions still roam and never know,
in their majestic power, of any weakness.

RAINIER MARIA RILKE

PROLOGUE

There was a river in a gorge far below the village which he suspected might be the Sepik, though the People called it Goubal, which meant simply, "dark river." He was trapped in a prison of infinite green mountain ranges, and in time he reflected that the body itself was a prison, and by extension the earth, though one large enough to amuse him for a lifetime if he could ever get to it. Once he asked Kopa ki if he had ever seen a water so large he couldn't see the other shore, and Kopa ki laughed and said that it was not possible, for if there was no other shore, what would keep the water from falling off the earth? And he reminded Russell of the great waterfall he had taken him to see below Runwarra. He said he had once met a man who told him about a water with no other shore, water bitter to the taste, flowing first one way and then the other, as if it didn't know in which direction its home was. Since the man was such a liar, Kopa ki had killed him and fed his brains to an opossum, then killed the opossum and burned it and buried its ashes deep in the ground. Kopa ki massaged one of the half-dozen pig tusk bracelets adorning his bicep as he told of it.

"No Quari," Kopa ki said, "there is no water greater than Goubal or its father, Runwarra."

There had been nights in the soaring shadow of the spirit house with its fires casting grotesque shapes, the drums thundering and flutes wailing, nights when that blood-drawn animal life had been his, filling him as the flutes were filled with the breath of others. It was a benediction of pure sensation without name or discernable form, and he had known a freedom not Kopa ki's, for whom the shapes and bones were powers which dominated his life and in turn portended to make him a specter to haunt his children, as a stern and jealous god might be thought to resent any joy not taken in his name and for his glory.

Russell noticed the skulls hanging from the rafters. They seemed to smile at him, their expressions changing in the firelight. Later he saw Kopa ki sleeping with the skull of his father propped under his head. Kopa ki believed the sight of its former skull would frighten his father's ghost and keep it from coming to take him to the land of the dead while he slept.

Unlike the skull of Kopa ki's father or the skulls and disjointed bones of other relatives which hung in net-like bags on the walls, the skulls in the rafters each had a rough hole in the temple.

"Maneowe," Kopa ki said when Russell pointed to a skull overhead. Kopa ki climbed up one of the casuarina posts which supported the thatched kunai grass and brought the skull down. "Maneowe," he said again, pointing at the splintered hole in the bony pate. "Maneowe."

Later, Russell learned that "maneowe" meant, "our food."

He heard the cries of strange birds and, in the first hour of darkness each night, the eerie, death-like cries of what he later learned was a flying fox. He heard drumming on hollow logs and mournful music. He saw a baby, Kopa ki's youngest son, Matu, curled up on a grass mat with the skull of his grandmother, and he saw Neggi, one of Kopa ki's wives, crouched in a corner of the hut with a baby in her arms. No, it wasn't a baby: it was a baby pig, and she was feeding it from her breast.

1

SHE KISSED HIM ON THEIR FIRST DATE. It wasn't that she allowed him to kiss her; he hadn't thought about it, hadn't let himself think about it because he knew thinking would make him nervous, lead him to say stupid things that would make him wish he were anywhere but in the front seat of his father's Ford, alone with her at that moment, his face burning self-consciously. But as it was, she leaned over the instant he'd pulled to a stop in the driveway and gave him a wet kiss on the lips. He'd turned to say goodnight, and she was there, supporting herself with one hand on the mohair upholstery, her face so close he could feel her breath, then kissing him as if they'd been together for years and it were the most natural thing in the world. It lasted only a few seconds. "Thank you, Russell," she said, "I had a nice time." Then she slid across the seat and opened the door.

When he got back home his head was still buzzing. He was elated and confused. She wasn't the kind of girl he'd suspected would even let him kiss her on the first date, but then he didn't have much experience with girls. But she *had* kissed him, and it was more than he could have dreamt. She likes me, he thought, or maybe she's teasing, though it didn't seem like that, or maybe she'd have kissed any boy with a car.

That was forty-eight years ago, and it still made his head ring with wonder and sadness when he thought of it. He pictured her white blouse in the darkness, moving toward the house, coming into the light from the porch. He'd sat watching her, the motor still running, waiting for her to turn and wave at the door, but she hadn't. She'd kissed him, then walked away. He could still smell her perfume, or thought he could, and they'd been married six months later.

IN 1940, WHEN RUSSELL WAS TWENTY years old and working in his father's lumber yard, the future seemed promising, or at least secure. There was some talk of the war, but nobody in Five Oaks believed America would get involved, or, if they did, no one said so. Russell's father, Daniel Wheeler, had fought in France and been awarded the Croix de Guerre for conspicuous bravery during a raid on the village of Ammertzwiller on the Alsace frontier with the French regiment to which he'd been assigned. He often told his son he'd gone off actually believing he was making the world safe for democracy, and in hindsight felt he'd only helped to make a greater mess. Daniel had returned to work in his father Cyrus' sawmill, and told Russell that sometimes in those first years home he would find himself out in the country, standing in a field or deep in the woods, having no idea how he'd gotten there. Two of his closest friends had been buried over there; they would never walk the streets of Five Oaks again, never have families or be anything but names on a plaque on the Soldier's Memorial. Their deaths had changed nothing; the same petty disputes waged among the same petty countries.

"If the combatants had settled it," Russell often heard his father say, "it could've been fair. We didn't want revenge. We didn't hate the Germans once the fighting was over. We felt sorry for them. We knew what they'd been through. We knew they could've been us. But Lloyd George and Clemenceau, no. Those bastards . . ."

Daniel Wheeler, with some capital from his father and a loan from the Bank of Five Oaks, started a lumber yard, selling oak and pine from the family sawmill as well as redwood from California and brick and hardware from the kilns and foundries of Chicago. Five Oaks had started its own cannery just before the war which, in the prosperity that followed, meant jobs for those in town and guaranteed markets for the growers who farmed the forest lands cleared in the lumber boom a few decades earlier.

Miriam was the kind of girl Russell had imagined for himself. She was beautiful and demure, yet mysterious. Her impulsive kiss, that night in the front seat of his father's Ford, sent him back to the Arthurian legends he'd read dutifully in school. He became fascinated with Guinevere and Iseult, and studied them as if they might be the keys to a treasure map. He dreamed of what ecstasy it might be to lie between Miriam's legs, silk curtains trailing away from the casements and clouds ghosting over the moon, angel voices. But why would she ever want to be touched by that crude thing he peed through? It was a world apart from grading and sorting lumber off the train or assembling truckload orders for contractors. So far apart, in fact, that he'd buzzed off the tips of two fingers in the band saw while cutting seven foot lengths of clapboard siding. It was a painful lesson in the separation of work and sex, and a vivid incentive to concentration until the night Miriam kissed his newly-healed fingertips and guided them under her skirt to the place where her body gave way. She shuddered as she had when he'd first touched her breast. He felt her breathing cut short in his ear. Miriam, grinding against his hand, moaning as if asleep and dreaming, wanting his hand there, actually wanting it. Incredible! He was careful not to wash his fingers and slept with them on his pillow, breathing in the scent of her powder and of something like the way the flesh of his arm had smelled when he'd sucked it for security as a child.

2

AFTER THE WAR, RUSSELL CAME BACK to a four-year-old daughter named Marlis and to a wife who was effectively a stranger. After years in the jungles of New Guinea, everything seemed strange. Five Oaks was like a town he'd read about in a novel, its people characters he distantly recalled. He'd had no communication with the world in which he'd grown up, no knowledge of who'd died, been born or married, who'd fallen on hard times, who'd prospered. Where he'd been and what he'd done seemed unrelated to either the war or to life anywhere else on earth.

All he knew for certain was that he didn't want to go back to selling lumber at the yard. He wanted to give himself to something, to be absorbed so completely that there wouldn't be time to reflect on how things had been or how they might've been. That feeling had been the genesis of Wheeler Industries. It wasn't ambition so much as restlessness, and the outlet he found for it was in the making of paper.

In the economy generated by the war, it was hard for a business not to succeed, and there was a greatly increased demand for quality finished paper. Letters, ledgers, books, pamphlets, fliers, house plans, contracts, magazines, billboards, laws—all required paper. And the second-growth timber that struggled back after Michigan was stripped bare by the lumber barons—the poplar and birch and scrub oak that grew up out of the ruins of what had once been thought an inexhaustible sea of primordial white pine—was more suitable and lucrative as pulp than as floor joists.

Russell's grandfather, Cyrus, through determined industry, integrity and civic-mindedness, had salvaged the family reputation from the calumny heaped upon his great-grandfather, Ambrose Wheeler. When he retired Cyrus left a few of his former hands to carry on, barely making their wages doing custom saw work. Russell took over the faltering mill, took a second mortgage on his house, and secured loans from the Bank of Five Oaks and the National Bank of Detroit with investments from his father and from several others who had prospered in canning, lumber or copper. He found Paul Blakely, a chemical engineer, through Michigan Agricultural College, and hired a young sales executive named Art Putney away from Georgia Pacific. Russell issued stock, made Art and Paul each three-percent owners, and bought secondhand pulping machinery and a new Fourdrinier machine for drying the pulp slurry into paper. He contracted for what farmers thought of as worthless trees and began buying up cheap forests of second-growth scrub.

By 1948 Wheeler Paper had a foothold in the Midwest and was paying small dividends to its stockholders. Some of the citizens of Five Oaks objected to the acrid smell created by the sulphate processing of the pulp, but the mill provided jobs and expanded business for the local merchants. Even those who'd originally raised their voices soon became accustomed to the smell, though it didn't enhance the occasional visitor's impression of the town.

In 1949 Miriam discovered she was pregnant. This came as a shock to both she and Russell, but by the time she gave birth to a son, Russell was so pleased by the idea that he went directly from the hospital to the mill and passed out cigars and popsicles to the workers and gave them the rest of the day off. He wouldn't think of taking time off himself while his employees were processing pulp, and he wanted to spend the day holding Miriam's hand and admiring their son Nick through the nursery glass.

In 1959 Wheeler retired its original bank debt and went on the New York Stock Exchange. By 1970 it owned 200,000 acres of Michigan forest land, the stock had split three times, and Russell was a wealthy man. By 1986 Wheeler Industries had purchased pulp plants and timberlands in Georgia and Washington state and employed over 7,000 people. Almost half the citizens of Five Oaks were stockholders and most of those who had gotten in early had become millionaires.

3

Russell lives alone now with Lily, his Labrador retriever. Josephine, who has been with him for thirty-five years, comes daily to cook and clean. He recently retired as Chairman of the Board of Wheeler Industries. According to the by-laws, as its founder he could have stayed in office till the age of seventy, and he isn't absolutely certain why he chose to step down on his sixty-fifth birthday. The reason he gave his board of directors was that he wanted to make room for a younger man with new ideas, but the truth isn't that simple. He can't ignore a feeling that time is getting short and there are other things he wants to do. And the business hasn't been as important to him as when it was untried and struggling and he knew each pulp-cutter and fork-lift operator by name. He's pleased to see the way the younger men are taking hold and curious about what Wheeler Industries will become, but whatever it becomes, it will be without him.

He lives in a big house on a small lake east of town, and he likes to watch the flights of waterfowl that come through in the spring and fall, the mergansers and buffleheads and goldeneyes, the Canadas and ringnecks and wood ducks, the scaups and occasionally a few pair of swans. He enjoys a glass of wine, and he listens to Vaughn-Williams, Oscar Peterson, and sometimes Miles Davis while the sun sinks down through the trees across the lake. Lesley, his daughter-in-law, brings him records and books she thinks he will like. She has worked for the county Department of Social Services for ten years and has just recently been named its director. She enjoys introducing Russell to many things he hasn't taken time for, and he looks forward to her visits. He is interested in those things which interest her because he loves her, and he loves her because she is the mother of his granddaughter, Katy. He frequently blushes at Lesley's attention and sometimes laughs when laughter is not quite called for. She is tall and slender with long, straight, auburn hair. She speaks very distinctly, almost as if she were trying to compensate for a slight impediment, and she has a lilt to her voice, a not quite placeable accent.

His son, Nick, seldom comes with her. Nick is sales services supervisor for the cardboard container division, a position he considers to be that of a glorified errand boy. He and Russell are not as close as Russell would like. Their relationship is polite but quite formal. Russell remembers a little blond boy who used to ride in front of him, his legs straddling the fuel tank of the Triumph motorcycle Russell owned back in the fifties. But Nick grew silent with adolescence, and it became a strain for them to talk about anything. Russell remembers the feel of the delicate rib cage he steadied with his left hand as he negotiated the corners of the section roads. Nick called it the "mona cycle." "Can we ride on the mona cycle, Dad?" Russell remembers how Nick's shoulders would hunch with excitement while he buckled the helmet strap under his chin, how he would tiptoe up to the machine as if it were a horse that might bolt and run away and have to be recaptured by stealth.

That was when he and Miriam lived together peacefully, though without great affection. After the war their life together had never been quite the same as in the year they'd shared before Pearl Harbor, when Russell's work had been satisfying but undemanding and each evening he'd looked forward to coming home. They'd been in love for that time, or had convinced themselves they were in love. On their wedding night Miriam discovered the birthmark on Russell's right shoulder, a perfect finger-sized crescent moon which she kissed tenderly, as if it were a piece of the true cross. Russell felt his life's ambitions fulfilled: he had a decent job with the prospect of one day taking over the lumber yard, and he had Miriam. Their marriage was a perpetual courtship; he was still amazed to have a woman so beautiful. There was a small lake east of Five Oaks where they dreamed of one day building a house, and often on summer evenings after work, Miriam would pack their dinner in a picnic hamper and they would drive out to the spot. There was a grassy knoll in a clearing overlooking the lake, and after dinner and a few beers, they sometimes made love on a blanket in the space they imagined might one day be their bedroom. Miriam would do things which filled Russell with amazement, things he had never imagined women taking pleasure in. Often at work he recalled Miriam's beauty in postures known only to him and felt elation. They had hardly been able to get enough of each other. They were thrilled by the idea that they could do whatever they wanted with each other, and that they could fall asleep in each other's arms.

4

Russell enjoys watching a sixteen millimeter film of Nick when he was three, taken on the dock in front of their newly-built house. Nick bounces and claps his hands to some unheard music. He approaches the camera and tries to look around it, to the left and then to the right. Finally he mouths, "Hi Dad!" and claps his hands for the joy of having discovered who is behind the whirring black machine.

Nick, however, remembers a bright winter afternoon on the frozen lake with his father, the wind tracing just an edge of sharpness on their faces, and the warmth of the sun covering them when they reached the lee of the winter trees. His father had chopped a hole in the ice with a spud, set down a green camp stool for Nick and handed him a short rod with lead sinkers, a bobber and a minnow already on the hook. "Now you keep your eye on this bobber," his father said. "It's your job to bring in anything that bites that hook." Then his father walked a hundred feet farther out on the lake and chopped another hole for himself.

Nick dropped the minnow through the hole and watched the bobber. The wind rippled across the hole and carried the bobber to the edge of the ice, then the weight of the sinkers called it back to the center again. He thought of it as a game the sinkers and the bobber were playing, or maybe it was the wind and the sinkers teasing the bobber. Whichever, he soon got bored and laid his rod down on the ice by the stool. The snow on the lake was crusty, and he found that after taking two steps he could slide a good ten feet. This was a much more interesting rhythm than that of the bobber: step-kick-slide, step-kick-slide. It almost made a kind of music, the rubber soles of his boots humming a diminuendo on the ice crust as he lost momentum. He spread his arms out for balance and imagined he was flying a rescue plane searching the arctic ice for the lost explorers, scanning the endless, endless arctic wastes. He was reaching the limit of his fuel, but maybe, maybe if he went just a few miles farther. . . . The wind over his ears joined in the chorus of triumphal music. The explorers were found. The brave pilot turned in a sliding arc and headed home. Now he was flying into the sun, and the glare of the ice made him squint. He looked down at his feet where the ice was darker, step-kick-slide, flying home, flying home, step-kick-slide.

He glanced up and saw his father dead ahead; he was almost on him. I must've gotten off course, he thought. But there were the trees close by and the green camp stool with the tear in the seat, and his father holding a fish, his fish, the one his bobber and sinkers had caught.

"Too bad," his father said, as he worked the fish free of the hook. "You were off playing around. This would've been the biggest fish of the day. If you had been paying attention like you were supposed to, this could've been yours." And he lowered the silver body back through the hole and let it go.

5

OCCASIONALLY RUSSELL GETS A LETTER from Miriam, and once in a while she calls. Their divorce was not bitter. Russell had been in love with his work and Miriam had grown bored. For a while she drank and then she began to create a life of her own. And when the children were grown she and Russell simply discovered they had nothing in common but some memories of the people they had been a long time ago.

Miriam found a younger man; her "puppy," Russell calls him. She helped him with his business, a chain of beauty salons. The puppy became quite famous for making formerly plain people glamorous. He gave several well-known actresses a new look to carry them into their golden years. Wayne, for he is known by his first name alone, has published several books about beauty, and frequently appears on afternoon television shows. He has, however, done little to alter Miriam's appearance, and she has kept her looks remarkably. She and Wayne were married ten years ago when she was fifty-four and he was thirty-nine. Russell went to the wedding. Nick attended dutifully, though his sister Marlis declined. It was at the Beverly Wilshire and there were features in the society pages and photos in *Women's Wear Daily*. Miriam's groom confided in Russell that he'd always admired more mature women. "I find them so soulful," he said over champagne and canapés. "So much life, so much depth of feeling." Russell nodded in agreement. He looked over at Miriam and wondered if they were discussing the same woman. Later, he wished her every happiness and asked her if she would now be called Mrs. Wayne.

When the phone rang Russell carried it to his leather over-stuffed chair, where he could watch the reflection of the evening sky on the dappled surface of the lake. "Well, how's retirement, Old Duck?" Miriam asked. "Are you driving everyone crazy?"

"You'd have to ask someone else about the crazy part, but I'm learning some things I didn't know. Owls, for example, hoot in the daytime, at least at this time of year. Did you know that? Maybe they're mating now. I heard them calling just a few minutes ago."

"Sounds like you're becoming quite the old hermit," Miriam laughed. Her voice had a kind of life he hadn't heard in their last years together.

"No, not really, though Marlis worries about me. She thinks I retired too soon. She probably thinks she ought to be running the mill, and she probably could. She calls from New York after every earnings report."

"Now don't be cynical."

"You know it's true."

"But how is it going, the company I mean?"

"Never better, really. You don't have to worry about your three percent. They don't seem to miss me much, though they're still kind enough to ask my advice."

"Maybe they figure you're just a cheap consultant."

"All I charge is my director's fee. But how are you and what's-his-name?"

"Now you are being cynical. Wayne is fine, and we're leaving for Europe next week. I called to let you know. We'll be gone three weeks. Wayne's doing shows with Yves St. Laurent in Paris and Rome and a competition in Frankfurt."

"Sounds exciting, especially Frankfurt."

"Well, I've never been to Frankfurt, so I wouldn't know. I wouldn't have picked it myself. Maybe I'll fall in love with it."

"I hope you do. Send me a postcard, and be careful. I mean it. Don't get kidnapped. Don't go anywhere alone."

"That's sweet of you darling. *I* mean it. And I will be careful. Give my love to Nick if you see him and to my precious little Katy. And to Marlis if she calls."

"I will." He was about to say good-bye, but he realized by the change in the sound of his voice in the receiver that there was no longer anyone else on the line.

6

THE GREEN DYE OF THEIR UNIFORMS was still wet when they stumbled off the planes in Port Moresby, New Guinea. The general staff had decided that khaki would be unsuitable camouflage in the jungle, and the day before they left Australia their fatigues had been dyed by a dry cleaner in Brisbane. The airplane ride from Australia had been the first for most of the National Guardsmen in Russell's regiment, and many of them, including Russell's boyhood friend, Roger Hatten, were sick from the turbulence, the close quarters, and the smell of the fresh dye in the overbreathed air. Despite such physical misery there was a general feeling of being off on an adventure. They were tough and confident, proven by the rigorous training they'd endured at Fort Polk and by their triumph in the month-long maneuvers in Texas. Russell felt as if they were on their way to more exotic maneuvers, to another camp where there would be no more arbitrary tests. The Japs, he was certain, weren't ready for the likes of the Red Arrow Division.

Russell's stomach dropped to his bowels and bounced back to his throat in the rough air over the Coral Sea. What made him more apprehensive than sickness, though, were the stories about the native Orokaiva spearmen in the Port Moresby area. In Brisbane his sergeant told him that the tribes were only half-converted from cannibalism. He explained to Russell that the tribesmen preserved fresh meat by tying a victim to a tree and cutting off pieces of flesh from his thighs and buttocks. They would slice off a succulent organ or an ear as a delicacy and then plaster over the wound with a pandamus leaf and keep their larder alive for

weeks so that he might witness his own body being de-
voured. Of course most of the Orokaivas had been con-
verted to Christianity, the sergeant assured him, though
they had retained a taste for white flesh.

Within a week of their arrival, Russell's company was
ordered out from Port Moresby to make a flanking movement over the Owen Stanley Range to the east of the main
advance. They followed a route which would later be
known as the Ghost Mountain Trail toward the Japanese
stronghold at Buna on the northern coast. It began as an
improved road to a rubber plantation at a place with a long
unpronounceable name beginning with 'K', which the soldiers from Michigan dubbed "Kalamazoo." Above the
plantation the road petered out to no road at all and then to
an indistinguishable trail, so that all vehicles had to be left
behind and they carried on with native bearers. Russell
wondered if these men might be cannibals and if there was
any way to tell short of being eaten by them.

There was mist in the foothills and in the light of the
moon it gave spectral shapes to the eucalyptus and to the
rubber trees hung with moss and vines. They heard a con-
stant dripping from the leaves which broke the eerie silence
at the higher elevations where no birds sang. This was not
at all how Russell had imagined the South Pacific. The
green dye that was supposed to make them inconspicuous
clogged the pores of the fabric and made the stifling heat
even more unbearable. The dye caused boils to erupt on
their skin, boils which were rubbed into bleeding sores on
the six weeks' trek over the mountains. Each day they
planned to make camp before the afternoon rains but were
invariably caught out by a sudden downpour, so that after
the first week they gave up any thought of ever being dry
again. Russell found leeches on his legs and stomach, and
learned to touch them with a lighted cigarette until they
gave up contending for his blood. The mosquitos came as
regularly as the darkness, and the men joked about how
much other life their blood was supporting.

One night Russell wept for Miriam and dreamt she was

there to comfort him, and in the morning he woke to find a small snake coiled under his pack. After that his homesickness subsided. The past became like a book, read once and now all but forgotten. There was no continuity to his experience, only isolated incidents in a world with no sky. Occasionally he would look up and catch a glimpse of sunlight through the tops of the intertwined trees, more the idea of light than light itself. One night by a stream he heard what sounded like a dog barking. Then it stopped suddenly, and he heard a noise like bundles of sticks being broken. In the morning he saw the tracks of a crocodile.

A week out on the trail, a platoon of Australian soldiers staggered down off the mountain, pale, emaciated and caked with blood. The two armies passed in silence, and Russell wasn't sure the Australians had even seen them as they stumbled by. Their appearence frightened the native bearers, and most of them deserted the following night. The trailside was littered with gear: socks, underwear, halves of blankets, mess sets, razors, anything that might lighten the load. Most of the men had discarded their steel helmets in favor of cloth campaign hats.

They followed the ridge of Ghost Mountain for two weeks, and at this higher elevation the heat gave way to an abiding chill. Most of the men had dysentery by this time, and for many of them the diarrhea was so virulent and so frequent that they simply cut the seats out of their fatigues rather than take the time to stop and pull down their pants. Russell had a fever and shivered almost constantly. He gave little thought to the Japanese. They seemed a remote enemy compared to the steep jungle terrain, the perilous cliffs along which he edged clinging to exposed roots and vines, the mud that slid constantly under his feet, the fever, the sores, the stench of his own excrement. The men gave up complaining and thought only of keeping up, as they'd been told that stragglers would invariably be shot by the Japanese.

In the third week they encountered a Japanese patrol, though Russell saw nothing of them. He heard bullets rattling through the palm fronds overhead and later saw his first corpse, a man from the 1st Platoon lying face down by the trail. Sickness and fatigue made him numb, and as he stumbled past the soldier he thought only, "dead body." Roger Hatten collapsed at the end of the day's march, and Russell cradled his head in his arm and tried to give him a drink from his canteen, but Hatten only choked as the water ran down his chin. He smiled at Russell and said, "Myra," before he died.

The "six o'clock" crickets began singing at dusk, and after dark the rains came. In some places where the trees were sheathed in moss, the canopy above glowed with a phosphorescence against the black sky. It reminded Russell of the fluoroscope machine in Bode's Shoe Store in Five Oaks, where he would peer down through a dark tunnel at the skeletal structure of his feet in the luminous pods of his shoes.

The men had all been curious about the enemy. Would their eyes have vertical pupils like those of a cat or a snake? Would they drool, and would their teeth be bucked as in the cartoon caricatures of Tojo? His first and only Japanese soldier came to Russell while his platoon was taking a ten minute break for cigarettes and C-rations before crossing a stream. Russell was lying on the bank drinking water that didn't have the metallic taste of his canteen, when he looked up and saw the bloated body float past. The dead soldier didn't look menacing. He looked like a balloon in the shape of a man. Russell and the other men on the bank watched him and said nothing. The body bumped a half-submerged log, spun slowly in the current and disappeared into the jungle downstream.

7

DURING THE FORTY-SEVEN DAY MARCH over the Owen
Stanleys, Russell had the abiding feeling that they'd been
cheated, lied to about combat and glory and esprit de corps.
They were being barraged by their bowels rather than by
the artillery that lit up the night sky. There was no night
sky, and nothing to fulfill his expectations: no adventure,
no enemy, no victories, no pliant Polynesian women to
adore him, only excrement and bad food and fevers and
sores, unbreathable heat and the clammy chill of Ghost
Mountain.

As a child Russell had often admired the plugged cannons
in the park, remnants of his father's war, and had incorporated them into his fantasies. Those imaginary battles had
been all-consuming and he had dreamed of another war to
bring them to fruition, or of an earthquake or a hurricane
or a great flood to disrupt the dreary routine of school and
church and chores. Later he remembered Nick's battles and
Saturday range wars and how, like those of his own childhood, they had been painless and without loss, unlike the
real war, which had been, for him at least, without glory or
any sense of victory.

When Nick's war came the illusory sense of "the great
adventure" had been destroyed through television, by the
numbing daily footage of fire fights and medivac helicop-
ters, of maimed veterans and napalmed children, of sum-
mary executions and self-immolating Buddhist monks, all
played out for the camera's eye.

Nick had spent his war as a transportation officer in Sai-
gon, shipping fresh bodies and munitions to places called

Plei Ku and Khe Sanh and Con Thien and reloading the cargo bays of C-5As with the tired and broken bodies of other young men, some in bags. He had felt no particular inclination toward military life, other than the unspoken expectation engendered by generations of photographs of Wheelers in uniform. But he harbored a belief that a commission might grant him the credentials of authentic adulthood, and since Michigan State was a land grant university where two years of ROTC were mandatory, the thought of not pursuing a commission was an option he hadn't consciously entertained.

The last six months of his tour were spent as the officer in charge of the Graves Registry, responsible for seeing that the bodies received in black, zippered bags were properly identified, repackaged in aluminum coffins and routed to the airport nearest their next of kin. Twice during this duty familiar names crossed his desk. One was Carl Purdy, a former high school classmate and the son of his family's dentist, whom Nick remembered chiefly by his locker room nickname, "Mr. Ed." Purdy had tripped a Claymore mine while walking point near Dak To, and that part of his lower anatomy once thought so equine was no longer available to aid in identification. The other acquaintance was Mark Bucholtz, a bunk-mate from Fort Riley, Kansas, who had cried himself to sleep through the first week of ROTC summer camp because he was convinced his girlfriend, the then-current Miss Ohio, was being unfaithful to him. Bucholtz had taken a round through his right cheekbone and appeared to be laughing on the half of his face still more or less intact.

During this time Nick stayed systematically stoned on percodan washed down with formaldahyde-laced beer. And when his time was up he returned to Five Oaks and transferred his practiced ennui to a job as an administrative trainee at Wheeler Industries.

In the stories Russell's father had told Russell and Nick, the war in France had seemed valiant despite the filth and discomfort. There were chain lightning artillery barrages, scouting patrols into no-man's-land, advances, retreats, the camaraderie of the trenches and the comforts of the villages when they fell back from the front. There was some affection in the way Daniel told of it, some humor. Most vivid was the story of a baseball game in Alsace when the company had been relieved from the trenches. The game had gone into infinite innings and had been a great amusement to the villagers. The diamond was set among stone buildings and many of the French and the soldiers who were billeted with them watched and cheered from the windows. A long barn served as a backstop behind the plate, and the only danger was in the outfield where the players were not sheltered by the dwellings. The game was called in the 16th inning when the right fielder, a corporal named Barney Tugood, dropped back for a long fly ball and was felled by sniper fire. Of course it was sad and tragic for Barney's folks back in Wisconsin, but to those who survived, it became a story to enliven a dreary campaign.

BELOW NATUNGA, ON THE FAR SLOPE of Ghost Mountain, there was a little bowl in the mountains, the dry bed of an old lake, a plain of kunai grass with a clear stream running through it, a bright green oasis in the amorphous jungle where the sun could penetrate all the way to the ground. Twenty years later, fishing a stream called Hellroaring Creek in the Absaroka Mountains of Montana, Russell thought of it again. He remembered the relief he felt resting there while his clothes dried in the sun. He shivered with the satisfaction of knowing that when he tired of catching cutthroat trout, he could walk back to his camp where Art Putney, Buck Leach and their guide would be waiting with bourbon and a hot skillet for the fish he would bring them, and that he wouldn't have to go back again down the trail toward Buna.

8

W HEN THEY WERE IN COLLEGE and Nick first phoned her, Lesley felt flattered although she hadn't seen or even heard of him before. She never thought of herself as being particularly attractive, and the idea that some boy who had seen her walking through the lobby of her dormitory cared enough to find out her name and call her up was thrilling. She had been tall since adolescence and her appearance in high school was gangly and stork-like. Lesley wasn't homely by any means, but thought of herself as big-toothed and awkward and had little confidence in her ability to attract men. She was unaware of the grace that had overtaken her by the time she was twenty, and never realized that her beauty and the intimidation of her stature, rather than awkwardness, kept her dateless.

Nick had joined his roommate, Bobby Termain, for dinner with Bobby's sister, Gail, at her dorm. They bought meal tickets at the dormitory office and found that the girls in the cafeteria line appreciated the novelty of male diners and favored them with extra helpings of everything, including dessert. As the only men dining in a room full of women, they felt like celebrities. They were savoring this intoxicating self-confidence on a couch in the lobby when Lesley walked by.

"Who is that?" Nick asked.

Gail shrugged. She was amused by the sudden worldliness of her brother's friend. "I suppose I could find out for you."

"Please do," Nick said.

Their first evening together began, not surprisingly, with

the tentative quality of a blind date. By the time they finished their strawberry sodas after seeing *The Brothers Karamazov* at the State Theater, they had worked through the usual questions of hometowns, majors and astrological signs, and were discussing the movie, which Lesley loved and which Nick found slightly depressing. They discussed the de-escalation of the war in Viet Nam, and Nick said he hoped it would be over before he graduated and took his ROTC commission.

What Lesley later remembered most vividly about the evening was that a freezing rain had fallen while they were in the theater and that Nick helped her into her coat and grasped her arm to steady her on the slick pavement and opened his car door for her. These were small courtesies he considered merely good manners meant to make a favorable impression, but Lesley had seldom felt so cared for or so important.

She had been born in Chicago but had only vague memories of her childhood there: an afternoon at the beach when her mother and father had swung her between them, breaking the incoming waves with her body as they waded out into the surf, the illuminated whiteness of the Wrigley Building at night, the quarrel to which she'd awakened one late spring morning, the crashing sound of dishes through the bedroom wall, her mother with a bleeding lip on the kitchen floor by the overturned table. All she remembered of her father was that he was tall, that he could lift her effortlessly to his shoulders, and that from up there the part in his black hair looked as white as the belly of a fish.

She brought a wet washcloth to her mother and helped her pick up what was left unbroken of the dishes and glasses. After that they moved to Nashville where her mother had been born, but Lesley didn't remember any relatives there, only a man she knew as Uncle Ned who sometimes spent the night in her mother's room. Her mother worked afternoons and evenings in a resturant, and Lesley usually saw her only in the mornings as she was getting ready for school. "I love you honey," her mother would say as she saw Lesley off down the block with her sack lunch. Once in a while, her mother walked Lesley the five blocks from their apartment to school and they shared a secret language while holding hands. Her mother would squeeze Lesley's hand three times, meaning, "I love you," and Lesley would squeeze her mother's hand four times, which meant, "I love you too." Her mother had begun to develop a gravelly whiskey voice, and Lesley preferred to remember her by these silent conversations of the hand.

One afternoon she came home from school and found her mother sitting at the kitchen table having a beer with a man named Al. Al was from Detroit, her mother explained. He was in Nashville on business and they had met at the restaurant. Al worked as a salesman for a Nashville company that made upholstery material for cars. He had a florid face and chubby red hands which Lesley detested. The hands were always reaching out to tickle or pinch her, and she didn't like to see them touching her mother.

Al laughed a lot. He told stories Lesley didn't think were funny. But her mother laughed, and Al laughed with her, and her mother said things like, "Al, you're a real pickle."

Al came for a visit every few weeks, and while he stayed with them, Lesley spent her afternoons at school and her evenings in her room reading Nancy Drew mysteries or *Treasure Island* or *My Friend Flicka* while Al and her mother watched television and drank beer. This continued after they moved to Detroit and her mother and Al got married. Only the books changed. As Lesley entered junior high she began reading Dickens—*Oliver Twist* and *David Copperfield*. She read *Huckleberry Finn, Jane Eyre* and *Wuthering Heights, A Member of the Wedding* and the stories of Flannery O'Connor, and her mother and Al kept on drinking. Her mother insisted that Lesley take Al's last name at school so that they would seem more like a family. Lesley hadn't cared about her name being Hubbard and didn't care if it was changed to Rawlings. In her mind it became that of the hero in each new novel she read.

One Friday afternoon in the fall of her senior year in high school, Lesley's English teacher, Miss Jenson, asked her to stay after class. Miss Jenson told Lesley she was impressed with the breadth of comparisons she had drawn in her paper on *Macbeth*, and with her insights and responses to questions in class.

"I think you could win a scholarship," Miss Jenson said. "I think you should enter the state essay contest. I'm sure you'd have a good chance of winning."

Miss Jenson helped Lesley select a topic—a comparison of the assassinations of Presidents Lincoln and Kennedy with the death of King Arthur at the hands of Mordred. Over her Christmas vacation Lesley devoted her energy to Mallory's *Morte d'Arthur*, Sandburg's *Lincoln*, and to commentaries on the Camelot years of the Kennedy administration. By immersing herself in other lives and times, she was able to block out, at least temporarily, the nightly battles between Al and her mother in front of the TV downstairs. Lesley sent her entry off to the judges in Lansing a week before the January 15th deadline. By early May, when it was announced that she had taken first place and won a full scholarship to Michigan State University, Al had moved out of the house and her mother had filed for divorce.

Lesley couldn't understand how her mother could've ever cared about someone like Al or why she would be unhappy about having lost him. While Lesley was trying to study, her mother would come into her room and talk about being lonely and about how Lesley's real father had been the only man she'd ever really loved and how rotten even he had been. Her speech would slur and become steadily less articulate until it degenerated into sobbing. Lesley would dutifully hug her mother, though she was repelled by the sodden smell of her, the mindless blubbering, the raccoon eyes and mascara-stained cheeks. Lesley felt ashamed of the impulse to shove her away and dreaded the idea of her mother coming to the award ceremony at the state capitol. She felt somehow responsible when her mother collapsed in a diabetic coma and had to be hospitalized three days before the Lansing trip, and wanted to deny the relief she felt that her mother wouldn't be going.

"I must be some kind of monster," she cried.

"You're not a monster." Miss Jenson took Lesley in her arms. "It's not your mother you despise, it's the demon that controls her. It's your mother's disease."

At the ceremony, Lesley received her scholarship from the Chairman of the Trustees of the University, and the governor congratulated her. Miss Jenson was thrilled with Lesley's reading of her essay, which concluded on the hopeful note that America provided the world's best hope for a truly free society, and came as close to the idea of Camelot as could be hoped in this imperfect world.

The drive home seemed to take no time at all. They had so much to say to each other, about the scholarship, the ceremony, and Lesley's future. Having a student so recognized was the crowning achievement of Miss Jenson's career. They were exhilarated when they arrived at the hospital to tell Lesley's mother about it and were met by the resident on duty.

"I'm sorry," he said. "Mrs. Rawlings lapsed back into a coma, and her heart stopped. We tried fibrillation, but she didn't respond."

Lesley noticed how he chewed his mustache as he paused between words, and that his shoes looked as if they had never been shined.

"I'm sorry." His tongue sought the corners of his mouth. "Your mother lapsed back into a coma. She suffered cardiac arrest. We tried fibrillation but . . ." The unpolished loafers appeared to be dancing.

9

LESLEY IS PLEASED WITH THE WAY Russell has taken to
the majestic melancholy of Sibelius. He tells her he imag-
ines deep mountain landscapes in the near dawn or near
dark. She has introduced him to Mahler, and together they
listen for the particular influences of nature in the *Third
Symphony*. Russell has been spending more time at home,
reading Thoreau's *Journals*, Whitman's poems and the nov-
els of Garcia Marquez, and wondering more and more
about what will happen when he dies. Each year now the
telephone brings him news of the death of men he has
known in the industry, men with whom he has bargained
and competed and with whom he has served on the boards
of corporations and trade associations. He has frequently
been called on to be a pall bearer for funerals in Five Oaks.
And now Boy Wheeler is dead. Russell has received a letter
from Boy's son, Cecil, whom he helped through medical
school and who is now a doctor on the Pine Ridge Indian
Reservation. He lays the letter aside as Lesley arrives, and it
occurs to him he won't be going back to South Dakota
again.

Three months earlier Russell had finally given in to Boy's
urging and cleared his calender to join him at Pine Ridge for
the annual Pow Wow and to see the work Cecil was doing.
There was a place Russell had read of near the town of Pine
Ridge, and when Boy took him there they sat in silence and
looked out over the rolling grass hills of the valley. The
road dropped down from the south, meandered below the
memorial chapel, climbed past a shack on the grade and dissolved into the ridge of the far slope. It was a hot afternoon

with a breeze too slight to matter and a lark sang somewhere above the brown summer grass. He sat there trying to imagine the place a century earlier, on a wintery day in December. Boy pointed out to him where the encampment had been, the direction from which the soldiers had come and the gully where the women and children had been mowed down by the Gattling gun.

"They believed the Ghost Dance would bring back the buffalo," Boy said. "It was the only hope they had for what had been their life. It was their religion, but they say that the dancing frightened the white people at Pine Ridge, so they wiped them out." The lay of the land couldn't have changed much. The chapel had been built and the cemetery, with a monument to those who had died there. One name, Ann T. Respects Nothing, recently painted on a crude wooden cross, amused both Russell and Boy. "She must have been something," Boy smiled, "some piece of work. I wish I had known her."

Across the valley, a huge white sausage-shaped propane tank, emblazened with red letters, screamed, "Wounded Knee" across the valley. They sat below the cemetery, feeling the pounding of the sun and siphoning what breeze there was from the grass. Russell looked up as Boy got to his feet. He thought Boy was going to say something, but Boy only shook his head. Then a moment later, he did speak.

"We can't be too sentimental about this here." He slipped his hands into the back pockets of his jeans and kicked at a clod of dry soil with the toe of his cowboy boot. "This kind of thing goes on happening. Some of those boys back at the Pow Wow talk about the villages they wiped out in Viet Nam; whole villages gone like that!" He brushed his palms together and let his right hand carry on toward the horizon. "They don't see it as being like this because the people were strange to them. It's sad they don't see it."

On the drive back to Pine Ridge, they talked about the drought and about how it might affect the pheasant population. It was the last afternoon they would spend together.

That evening Russell drove to Rapid City to catch his flight home, and now, three months later, this letter from Cecil that Boy was gone.

EVERY AUTUMN RUSSELL HAD DRIVEN WEST with Art Putney, Paul Blakely and sometimes with Warren Riorden, his physican from Grand Rapids, or Buck Leach, president of Five Oaks Mutual Insurance, to go pheasant hunting with an Indian farmer named Russell Wheeler near Pierre, South Dakota. It was a ritual that began as an adventure in 1955 when Art showed Russell a story in *Field & Stream* about the open spaces and almost limitless hunting on the eastern great plains. Pheasants thrived in the corn and prairie country, and it sounded like the perfect excuse for a long weekend getaway. "I can't think of one good reason not to," Russell said when he handed the magazine back to Art on a Monday morning in late September. "But do you think the company could spare all this executive talent for three or four days?"

"Hell," Art smiled. "I expect the place would be more efficient without us, don't you?"

They drove north in Russell's big DeSoto Town Car, their duffels strapped down to the roof rack with a brown canvas tarp, and caught the C&O ferry at Ludington. Buck Leach passed his flask around as they stood at the rail and watched the bow waves curl over the calm blue water of a brilliant Wednesday in October. The Michigan shoreline was fading behind them, Wisconsin and all the rest of America lay ahead, and the bite of the whiskey on their tongues, before noon and on a weekday, gave them a tremendous sense of freedom. They docked at Kewaunee about noon, and when the car was unloaded, they headed west through a land of rolling hills and picture-book farms. It was a tamer country, more settled than that from which they had come, Russell decided, a land with all the rough edges sanded off.

Crossing Wisconsin, they talked about the merger of the AFL and the CIO and wondered what that might mean for union activity at the mill. They talked about the Supreme Court ordering desegregation of schools in the South and about a black man named Martin Luther King they were starting to see on the TV news. It was dark when they stopped in Mankato for gas.

They checked in at the Prairie Home Guest Cabins near Pierre early the following morning, took a two hour nap, found a diner called Carter's Cafe at the edge of town and had breakfast. They'd only had ham and baloney sand- wiches in the car.

"I'm hungry enough to eat my boots, if they were fried up just right," Warren said. He rubbed his hands together as his words steamed out into the crisp morning air.

They got directions to a sports shop from a waitress at the cafe, and while they were buying their non-resident li- censes Russell inquired about where they might find good places to hunt.

"Well." The owner of the sports shop scratched his head. "The best thing is just to drive along the road till you see a cornfield that looks good to you, and then ask the farmer for permission to hunt. I would ask though. Some of these boys are pretty territorial. Sometimes it greases the skids if you slip them a buck or two." He looked down at the coun- ter on which Russell was filling out his license form. "Wait a minute," he said. He turned the form around so he could read it right side up. "Your name Wheeler?"

"Yes it is. Did I do something wrong?"

"No, nothing wrong. Russell Wheeler?"

"That's right."

"Well, what do you know about that?"

"Know what?" Russell felt a bit confused.

"There's a Russ Wheeler about ten miles west of here, an Indian fella, got some dandy fields. I expect he'd get a kick out of you guys, I mean with your name being the same and all. I'd give him a call for you, but he doesn't have a phone. Go on out there and tell him Barney Metcalf sent you."

"Well that'll be great, Barney. Thanks. I've never known another Russ Wheeler. What kind of Indian?"

"Sioux. Oglala Sioux."

"You mean like Sitting Bull?" Buck asked.

"Yeh, like that," Barney smiled. "But his wife's the real warrior. You go on out there. You fellas'll get a kick out of Boy Wheeler all right."

"NO SHIT?" SOUTH DAKOTA RUSS WHEELER said when Russell introduced himself. South Dakota Russ was dark and moonshaped and filled the doorway of his paintless house. His clothes notwithstanding, he looked like an Indian Russell had seen in the movies. His grip was hard and muscular, and Russell had the feeling he was shaking hands with a tree.

"Mama, get this," he yelled over his shoulder. "Russ Wheeler's here."

"What are you saying?" The voice was deep and resonant. It sounded more as if it should have come out of the man in the doorway than from the pale thin woman who walked up behind him. "You flipped or something?" She was drying her hands on a soiled dish towel.

"No. I said this here's Russ Wheeler and his friends from Michigan. They're out here hunting pheasants."

"So you're Russ Wheeler?" She edged her husband aside and took control of the doorway.

"Yes Ma'am," Russell smiled and nodded. "That's what it says on my birth certificate. And this is Art and Buck and Warren and Paul." He turned to indicate the men standing behind him.

"Well I got a paper that says we're married," she said, and laughed. "What do you think about that?"

"Well, I, ah . . ." Russell blushed. "I guess the luck would be all mine."

"You're okay," the woman said. She tossed back the hair that was hanging over one eye. "Come on in."

She had a gaunt look about her. Her cotton dress hung

shapelessly from her bones and emphasized the paleness of her freckled skin. Her mannish brogans clomped on the boards as Russell followed her down the dark corridor, and for that moment he was in love with her. He wanted to lift her from what he saw as the bleakness of her life, hold her head in his hands and tell her she was beautiful, and please her out of any context she could know, just for that moment, as he watched her enter the light of the room at the end of the hall.

The kitchen was reasonably well kept, but what struck Russell and his friends and what caused them to exchange glances of surprise was that there was almost nothing in it that they would call furniture, in their sense of the word. The table was constructed of inch-thick oak planks, nailed down over sawhorses. Overturned packing crates stenciled with Allis Chalmers and Mitchell Co-op served as chairs, and the kitchen cupboards were orange crates placed on the counters and filled with dishes and glasses, thick porcelain coffee mugs, baking soda and cereal boxes.

"You can call me Boy," South Dakota Russ said as his wife poured coffee from a blue iron pot. "Everybody does around here. And the boss lady here is Myrna." He nodded toward his wife, who looked as if she were smiling to herself over some private joke as she set the coffee pot back down on the woodstove.

The hunters all nodded in appreciation and sat tentatively on the overturned crates like adults at a childrens' tea party.

"What do you do back in Michigan, Russ?" Boy Wheeler asked.

"I'm in the timber business," Russell said. "We make paper."

"I guess there's a lot of that back there," Boy said. He lit a cigarette and nodded as if he were agreeing with himself. Russell could hear Arthur Godfrey murmuring from the radio in the corner of the kitchen, though nobody seemed to be listening. "Timber I mean," Boy added. "You can see there ain't too many trees around here." He tossed his head toward the back of the house. "Are you the Wheeler from Wheeler paper?"

Russell stared at him and nodded.

"No shit? I know about that." Boy got up from the table, reached up on top of one of the orange crates behind him and pulled down a white box with a label on the end that said "Wheeler Bond" in red letters and had an outline map of the lower peninsula of Michigan on it. "Well damned if I'm not pleased to meet you," Boy exclaimed.

"You already said that Boy." Myrna was shaking her head. "Mr. Wheeler here is Mr. Wheeler wherever he goes. It ain't no surprise to him."

"Well I'm still damned pleased to meet you. I keep my feathers in this box," Boy said with pride. "I use it 'cause it's got my name on it. And yours."

"Feathers?"

"Yeh. Feathers I find." He took the lid off the box and tilted it up so they could see. "I think there's a reason for every feather. Some reason the bird dropped it for you where you find it. It's kind of like collecting messages, pieces of luck. This here's an eagle feather." He laid down a brown feather with small white plumes at the quill. "This is a red-tailed hawk, this a crow. Mind if I hunt with you guys? I could show you some good spots."

"We'd be honored," Russell said. He looked at Art and Buck and Warren and Paul, and they smiled over their good fortune.

"That's great," Art chimed in.

"I think there's some kind of real luck that brought us here," Russell said, "like the luck of your feathers."

"This makes me happy," Boy said, and Russell was moved by the innocence and generosity of the man.

Boy and Myrna insisted that Russell and his friends check out of the guest cabins and put up with them. At first they were reluctant, but they were won over by Boy's sincerity and by the effort Myrna put into the dinner she fixed for them after their first morning's hunt. Russell insisted that he and his friends buy the groceries during their stay. Boy could barely feed his family, let alone five wealthy hunters from out-of-state. Their shopping ensured food a little more to their liking, because in truth Myrna was not one of the world's or perhaps even South Dakota's great cooks. Paul, who served as camp cook during deer season in Michigan, did what he could to spice up the stews and to minimize the indigestion. They spread their sleeping bags in the loft of the barn. The accommodations were considerably more rustic than the Prairie Home Guest Cabins, but they were mellowed significantly by a liberal treatment of Boy's home brew. The straw in the loft was clean and the pungent smells of pigeon, rain-spoiled hay and manure that wafted up to them as they settled in after a long day's hunting completed the fantasy that their trip to South Dakota was a journey in time.

The stories they brought home were less of bagging limits and making remarkable shots than they were of Boy's passing the jug around the table after dinner and of how each of his boys took their token hit off it.

"That stuff would close my throat right up and turn my eyes half way around," Russell told Miriam and Marlis and Nick as Josephine served him another slice of Yorkshire pudding from a silver-handled dish. "And little Cecil would lay it over his shoulder and take a slug and hardly even blink." Russell felt slightly silly as he told the story, dining in the formal luxury of the silver candelabra and crystal goblets Miriam had collected as the company flourished.

He told how Boy left the Pine Ridge Reservation during the war and met Myrna at a U.S.O. dance in Georgia, near Fort Benning. Myrna's maiden name had been Wheeler, and after the war, when they decided to marry, he had taken her family name because she refused to live on the reservation, and they knew that with a last name like Running Boy, life would be tough for their children in a white man's school.

"When I was little," Boy explained, "I used to run everywhere. I had so much energy I thought I would go crazy. So they called me Running Boy. That's the name they gave me, but Chief Horn Cloud told me my real name could only be known by the course of my life and that it would probably never be spoken. Maybe it's best it's a secret, but I wonder sometimes what it is."

"Your name's like that, Russ," Boy said one evening as they emerged from the last cornfield and turned up the section road toward Boy's house. "Maybe it's Makes Much Paper, but I don't think so. Maybe at the end of your life you'll know who you are. My grandfather's name was Moccasins That Don't Touch The Ground, because he went everywhere on horseback, even into church once, they say, and my father's name was Oliver Moccasins That Don't Touch The Ground. But he almost never rode a horse, and when I came along they figured that name was just too long anyway. So now we're just a couple of guys called Russ." Boy had a brace of pheasants slung over his left shoulder, and Russell noticed how the blood stains had blackened the canvas of his hunting shirt.

THE STORY ABOUT SOUTH DAKOTA that Nick asked Russell to tell again and again was the one about the snakes. There were lots of snakes in South Dakota, lots of rattlers, people said, and you had to think about them as you spread out to hunt a field. You shouldn't be preoccupied with them, but you had to keep in mind that they might be there, soaking up the last warmth of the autumn sun before slithering down into a prairie dog den for the winter.

One day Russell and Boy were off hunting alone together near a dry stream bed at the edge of Boy's farm. They kicked two pheasants up out of the corn and watched them glide over a field of brown grass and settle in near the cottonwoods along the bank of the dry wash. Under his flannel shirt Russell could feel drops of perspiration sliding down over his ribs. He didn't much care whether they got the birds or not, but he couldn't tell Boy. For all he knew, Boy might've felt the same way about it and couldn't tell him. It was a point of hunting etiquette neither of them was prepared to breach, and their pride forced them on into what had become an armed march in the unseasonable heat.

A cicada was whining somewhere in the cottonwoods, and its noise may have covered the noise of the snake, which Russell didn't hear until it was almost underfoot. He saw the quivering tail at the same instant he heard its rattle, and jumped backwards instinctively before he could even form the word "snake" in his mind. He was out of striking range when he came back to earth, but he experienced a chill so violent that he felt the sweat freeze on his skin as he stared at the big diamondback, its head arched menacingly, its tongue searching out the smell of him. It took Russell half a minute to work up enough spit to call out. "Ba . . . Ba . . . Boy," his voice cracked, "Over here!" Later he wondered why he hadn't simply embellished the animal with two barrels' worth of birdshot.

"That's a big one," Boy said when he reached Russell's side. He was short of breath, and he wiped the sweat off his face with a red bandana. "You step on him, it'd be like stepping on a land mine. That one's a killer."

"Should I blast him?"

"No. I don't think so. I think maybe my son's around."

Russell watched as Boy pulled something up out from under his shirt, something white and slender like a pencil attached to the leather thong around his neck. He put it to his lips and made a shrill high-pitched whistle. "Eagle bone," Boy said. He held it up for Russell to see before dropping it back down his shirt.

"Now what?" Russell asked.

"Time." Boy said. "See what happens."

The whining of the cicada and the buzzing of the rattler blended into what was more a color than a sound. It was the color of heat, the color of the parched grass, of the dry riverbed and the mottled skin of the snake. Even the breeze that stirred the dry leaves in the cottonwoods cooled nothing, changed nothing. It was all the more brown for the color of the sky, the brilliant, infinite blue meeting the rise of the dry wash. The two Russells stood listening to the grass and the trembling leaves, hypnotized by the immutability of the day and by the menacing poise of the rattler. They heard hoofbeats, or maybe only felt them in the ground. Russell thought he could still hear the scream of the eagle bone, but of course he couldn't. Cecil appeared in the heat waves above the ridge and the black-and-white paint horse floated up under him, bareback, galloping over the hill. The horse and rider took a long time to reach them, though they weren't far away.

The horse was lathered when Cecil reined it in; it snorted and pawed as if standing still were an unnatural act. "What's up?" Cecil asked.

Boy pointed to the rattler. His son nodded and began unbuttoning his shirt, and for a moment it seemed to Russell that Cecil was stripping down to grapple with the snake. As Cecil peeled his shirt away, it looked as if he were wearing a girdle around his ribs, a yellow and reddish girdle. He quickly unwound it, and suddenly Russell saw a five-foot king snake in the boy's hands. Cecil leaned down and dropped the king snake on the ground, and before Russell understood what was happening, the snakes were thrashing furiously in the dust. He could see the rattler striking ineffectually, the beautiful king snake wrapped around it like a sheath.

Russell didn't know if it lasted a few minutes or an hour. The cicada continued, and its song grew more distinct as the battle subsided and the rattler was silenced. The king snake had its coils around the rattler's throat, or where Russell imagined its throat might be. Then Cecil was on the ground, the heel of his boot on the rattler's head, a snake in each hand, pulling them apart like tangled ribbons. He held the rattler up so they could see.

"A big one," Boy said.

Cecil dropped it to the ground where it coiled and twitched in death. He handed the king snake to his father. "Hold this while I mount up," he said.

"I'll bring this dead one along," Boy said. "It'll make a nice hatband."

Cecil grabbed the horse's mane and leapt up onto its back. His father handed him the king snake, and he took it in both hands. He held it against his torso, and it wrapped itself around him and became a girdle again.

10

Russell was troubled by something he had read in Thoreau. He was troubled because he had found a kind of peace in Thoreau that made sense to him. *How few things can a man measure with the tape of his understanding.* All his life had been given to figuring things out, and in business it had worked well for him. But he couldn't figure out getting old; he couldn't figure out dying. *How many greater things might he see in the meanwhile.* Russell wondered how Lesley, having just turned thirty-seven, could understand what had only recently begun to trouble him. He was amazed to discover that Thoreau reminded him of things he once knew and had forgotten, that the words on the page seemed to be coming not into him but out of him, as if he, Russell Wheeler, invented them as he read. He was grateful to Lesley for making him listen and wondered if anyone else could have done this, could have brought him to Whitman and caused him to regard the grass he would someday become as more than something to mow or play golf on. He had begun to regard these voices as old friends, but today he felt accused by them.

Lesley poured coffee into the blue porcelain mugs and took a seat cross-legged on the floor in front of his chair. The word "despoil" had stuck in Russell's craw.

"Thoreau says that if he spends the day in the woods, just because he loves to be there, that people think he's an idler, but that if he spends the day figuring how to despoil the woods and turn them to a profit, he's considered an industrious man."

Lesley held the mug in both hands and listened through the steam which rose from the coffee.

"But how does he think people live on this earth? Where does he think the wood for those pencils he made and sold came from? What about the wood he burned in his fireplace or the trees he cut down to build his cabin? If everybody lived like he did, we'd all starve to death."

Lesley's deep brown eyes followed his thoughts, and Russell began to feel a little foolish. From the kitchen where Katy was watching *Sesame Street*, they could hear Big Bird talking.

"I don't know, Russ," Lesley responded. "I think he was talking about appreciating the world for what it is rather than for what we can make out of it. Why take it so personally?"

"I've been cutting trees for forty years now, millions of them. We maybe even made the paper this book is printed on. But I never thought I was despoiling the woods. And it wasn't just money. It's what I did every day because I didn't know what else to do."

"So you've done something important, provided jobs for thousands of people. We live in a physical world."

"And we reforested," Russell continued. "It's not like we've denuded the state of trees."

"Okay, okay!" Lesley held up her hands. "I grant you absolution."

Russell smiled and shook his head. "I'm sorry. I got carried away."

Lily got to her feet from where she lay curled at the end of the couch, turned a slow circle and flopped back down with a deep groan.

"Are we disturbing you, old girl?" Russell nodded in her direction. "Lil has the final word on all this philosophy. Food and sleep and a little love."

"Thoreau can be a bit of a prig sometimes." Lesley got up and sat on the arm of Russell's chair. "I confess I'm a lowly, sensual creature." She bent down, kissed him on the

forehead and laughed. "We still love you, Russ. You looked
like a little boy there for a minute."

Russell felt himself teeter on the edge of something he'd
avoided, the way a reformed drunk avoids the smell of al-
cohol. His breath backed up in his chest. "I guess I felt like
one."

"Nick used to look that way sometimes," Lesley mused.
"He used to be so sensitive about what he thought I was
thinking. If I wasn't smiling he thought it had to be something he'd done, or hadn't done. I'd get so damn tired of
smiling, just trying to keep him happy. I'd feel like one of
those twits in the Miss America Pageant. Now it doesn't
seem to matter anymore."

"I never quite know what he's thinking," Russell said.

"When I was carrying Katy," Lesley continued, "he told
me he felt left out. I'd been trying to get pregnant for ten
years, and I wanted to share it with him, but he got so quiet
and withdrawn. He said he felt like I was having an affair
with this thing inside me and didn't love him anymore. But
I did love him. I told him this 'thing,' as he called it, was his
as much as mine, a part of him also. I thought that after
Katy was born he'd be happy, but it's as if he resents her,
and resents me, too, like he wants me to choose, him or her.
But there isn't any choice."

Russell remembered how he and Nick had passed like
ghosts in the house, how Nick, coming home from a date,
would sneak through the kitchen to avoid passing Russell's
desk where he might be talking letters into the dictaphone,
how he'd hear Nick in the hall but wouldn't call to him,
how he'd think to ask Nick about school but couldn't remember what subjects he was taking. When Nick was playing football and Russell asked him if he was going to start,
Nick resented it because he hadn't started. Russell had
meant to seem interested but instead had sounded
accusatory.

"I didn't spend enough time with him," Russell said. "I
didn't come home early enough or often enough. Miriam

hired lots of help and then found she didn't have anything to do. I think Nick probably thought Josephine was his mother."

"Is that what happened with you and Miriam?" Lesley asked.

"I liked to think so because it allowed me to resent her. I could think she just didn't appreciate what I was doing. But it went further back than that, to the years she spent thinking I was dead. Suddenly I was back and everything had changed. I think she'd fallen in love, or half in love with someone else. Knowing Miriam, I can't imagine her waiting around. She thought she was free and she'd become hard somehow."

"And you had Marlis then?"

"We had Marlis. I'd never even heard of that name. She was four years old, and I was supposed to jump right in and start being a father. And then Nick came along. He was so cute." Russell smiled. "Sometimes I wish I had him back the way he was. I wish I could've felt about him and Marlis the way I feel about Katy. But that kind of regret's all wasted."

"And now?" Lesley asked.

"I don't know," Russell sighed. "Nick's not happy, I know that. He thinks I pressured him into the company. I tried not to. I honestly did."

"I think he's seeing someone," Lesley said. "It's just a feeling I have, the way he closes me out. He hasn't paid any attention to me, as a woman I mean."

Russell straightened himself up in the chair.

"I mean he hasn't made love to me in over two years."

"He's a fool!" Russell exclaimed. He stroked Lesley's cheek.

"I know," she said. "I almost don't care."

Russell could see her eyes brighten with tears. "Sometimes a man can forget his wife is a separate human being and not some extension of himself. I know I find Miriam more interesting now she's not mine anymore."

They heard Katy's sneakers squeaking on the hardwood

floor. "Hey Gamp, were you ever a bird?" She walked to him and crawled up on his lap.

"Was I ever a bird? Well, not that I can remember. Why?" Russell laughed.

"Is Big Bird a bird?"

"Well, he's supposed to be."

"But is he really?"

"Well no, I think he's really a person in a bird suit."

"Oh." Katy started unbuttoning his shirt.

"Hey, what are you doing?" Russell asked.

"Taking your clothes off."

"But I'll get cold." He put his hand over her hands where they were working on a button over his sternum. "Why are you taking off my clothes?"

"Maybe you're a bird in a people suit." Katy giggled and held her hands up over her mouth.

"He's really a bear," Lesley said. "See all the fur on his chest."

Katy grabbed a handful of the grey hair beneath Russell's unbuttoned shirt. "Then he's a polar bear, Mom," Katy said. "An old white polar bear."

11

Russell had some questions about Tom Carey, the man he had chosen to take his place as CEO of Wheeler Industries. He had confidence in Tom's abilities and was pleased with the hard decisions he had made in streamlining the corporate staff, but worried that Tom might be a little too demanding on his co-workers (Russell didn't like the term subordinates). He was worried about morale.

Russell wondered if it might not be his own attitude, if he might resent anyone who took his place, especially someone as brilliant as Carey, a Harvard MBA who had come from Pacific Packaging when Wheeler acquired it seven years earlier. Carey was often mentioned in the society pages of the Detroit and Grand Rapids papers as an eligible bachelor, and Russell had noted that he had recently been seen escorting the the governor's ex-wife.

He isn't a regular company man, Russell thought, but he's made a success of everything we've thrown at him. Of course any man who fights his way to the top of a major corporation is likely to be a bit egotistical. If he didn't have confidence in himself he couldn't expect others to. But Russell was beginning to wonder if Tom Carey might be a little too confident.

"I've worried about that," Art Putney said when Russell asked his opinion. They sat in Art's office and talked across the jumble of print-outs, memos, letters and trade journals that obscured the mahogany surface of Art's desk. It always amazed Russell that Art ever found anything or got anything done with that much clutter before him. Art was now vice-president of marketing and still had two years until his mandatory retirement.

"You can't argue with his performance. He's reorganized the container division, got that mess straightened out, and we've got a record year going." Art coughed, wiped his mouth with his handkerchief and continued. "He's smart, I'll grant you that, and he's a hard driver. He pushes himself as hard as he does anyone else. It's not a problem for me, but he intimidates the hell out of some of the younger guys." Art got up, walked around his desk, and sat in the chair next to Russell's. "I think it's more a matter of style than anything else. He's so damn bright. You know there aren't many companies this size where everyone calls the boss by his first name or can walk into his office and talk to him the way we could with you. That kind of thing changes with professional management. We were all closer in the early days, but we're a big company now. I try to keep that in mind."

"I'm trying, too," Russell said. "I miss the kind of spirit we had when we were thrilled at every little success. But you can't give a man a job and then try to tell him how to do it. I won't be guilty of that."

"I know," Art acknowledged.

"And I don't want the job back." Russell laughed. "I must say that I'm enjoying my new life."

"I'm happy about that." Art reached out and squeezed Russell's shoulder. "You're setting me a good example, as always."

"You know that I'd thought about you or Paul for the job, but you guys just wouldn't have been around long enough."

"I think you picked the right man. I think he has vision. I think those people who are uneasy about him are probably the ones who ought to be."

"What do you think about Nick?" Russell had hoped to toss off the question in passing, but he recognized the solemnity of feigned indifference in his voice.

"Well Russ, we've been together a long time." Art coughed and held his fist to his lips as he cleared his throat.

"Art, I want to know what you think."

"Nick's a fine boy." Art paused. "God it's hard to be honest."

"I know." Russell nodded, and they both smiled with relief.

"His heart just isn't in it. We've been carrying him along. I've kept hoping he'd find a place and dig in. But I don't think it's going to happen. Nick's messed up, that's all. If he was somebody else it might be okay. But people can't forget who he is. And he can't either."

Russell got up, walked to the window, and looked down into the receiving yard of the mill. "I guess I've known that all along. I don't know what I could've done to make it any different. I had myself believing that if I didn't think about it, it wouldn't be that way."

LATER THAT AFTERNOON , Russell walked into the kitchen and found Josephine on her knees, scrubbing the lower oven. He asked her if there was any coffee.

"It's in the pot," Josephine said. She sighed with disgust at having to state the obvious. She was working on the remnants of baked-on grease the self-cleaning oven never quite seemed to burn off, and there was something about the way she kept scrubbing and didn't turn to look at him that made Russell wish he hadn't asked. He poured the steaming coffee into an indigo mug and wondered if his concerns about Tom Carey weren't just a way of hunting trouble. Maybe I don't have enough to do, he thought. Russell had sensed a tone of resignation in Nick's voice when he'd phoned to ask him to come by to talk about something important. Nick told him he was catching a plane to New York but that he'd stop on his way to the airport.

An hour later in his den, Russell asked Nick the same question he'd put to Art Putney about Tom. He'd meant to talk with Nick about what he was doing now and what els he might do, to let Nick know he was interested and maybe get him to start talking. But with Nick standing there in front of him the real question—whatever it might've been—didn't come to him. He noticed, as he often had, how much Nick's gaze resembled Miriam's, the same longing stare that seemed to look beyond what was before it as if for something more worthy of its attention. Nick wasn't quite as tall as Russell but he looked taller because of his slender build. He was handsome, but there was some lack of resolution about his features which reflected his indecision about life, and made him appear not quite focused.

"I wanted to get your opinion about Tom Carey," Russell began. "I wanted to get your view of the kind of job he's doing." Russell paused a moment to see if there might be some response, but Nick continued to stare at him as if still waiting for the question. "It's only a feeling I have," he went on. "He's accepted directorships on the boards of three other companies since he became chairman, and I'm beginning to wonder if he can spread himself that thin and still do a good job for us." He wondered why he was asking Nick this. The words had come out him as a way of conquering the silence.

Nick shrugged and rolled his eyes, as if he couldn't believe he'd come all the way out to his father's house for this. "Why are you asking me?" His voice was deep yet still had a slightly adolescent adenoidal quality.

"Because I value your opinion."

"He's treated me okay." Nick looked at his watch. "But then my name's Wheeler."

"Do you think that's made a difference?" Russell felt this might be an opening.

"Well, obviously he isn't going to fire me." There was a note of resentment in the way Nick said it.

"Well, look at it this way." Russell paused and realigned the stack of magazines on the coffee table between them. "Do you think he's doing a good job, generally? Do you think he's giving the right kind of leadership?"

"I don't know." Nick smiled derisively. "That's not my job."

"What would you do about it if you were me?" Russell realized, as soon as he had asked it, that it was a stupid question.

"I'm not you." Nick tugged at his collar.

"I'm just trying to understand the situation. I wanted your view on it."

"It's not my business. I've got a plane to catch," Nick said abruptly. He picked up the raincoat he'd dropped over the couch. "I've got errands to run."

"Errands?" Russell asked.

"I have to sharpen the pencils for the sales meeting in New York."

"Is that how you think of it?"

"That's the way it is." Nick's voice was emphatic.

"Thanks for coming by."

Nick said nothing.

"I appreciate your time."

Nick shrugged his shoulders, turned and walked out of the room.

Russell sat on the arm of the couch as if he were waiting for something to happen. Then he got up and walked over to the CD player, switched on the amplifier and put a Sibelius disc in the machine. He walked over to the window that looked out on the lake, collapsed in his rocker and sat listening to the pensive awakening of the opening movement.

12

Y EARS AFTER HE HAD RETURNED from New Guinea Russell would read of the Buna campaign and find it hard to believe there had been a great battle there. It was like reading a history of another time. He had been airlifted from Wanigela with malaria and dengue fever before his regiment ever reached Buna, and his plane crashed in the mountains somewhere southwest of Natunga. Russell determined this much from the maps Kopa ki had rescued with him from the wreckage of the C-4. He had come to think of the tribe as the Goubal, from the name of the nearby river that ran through the gorge below the village, though they called themselves Minarri, which meant the People. The People regarded the wrecked plane as a gift from the gods. Russell had been the sole survivor, and they deemed him the bringer of these treasures from the sky—silk parachutes and the boots and clothing they had removed from those bodies not burned in the wreckage—which they incorporated into their wardrobes of egret feathers, boar tusks and the long dry gourds they wore over their penises. Several of the men took to wearing shorts or trousers with their penile gourds protruding obscenely through the unbuttoned flies. There were a few tins of various pills and an M1 rifle, but no ammunition had been found. The idea of trying to explain a rifle to the People with no way to demonstrate its powers amused Russell.

As he learned their language through Kopa ki's regular practice of pointing and pantomime, he discovered that the People thought airplanes and the mysterious things associated with them were gifts the white man had received first but which would eventually come to them. As the guardian of this first installment of their gift, they believed Russell had been born from the dead, and regarded his illness as a recovery from the trauma of birth.

At first he had mistaken the plane's rapid loss of altitude for another symptom of his fever. But when he saw the fear on the face of Larval Thompson, the medic who had been attending him, he realized the rush he felt in his stomach wasn't his alone. Russell crawled to a window and saw the starboard engine in flames. His head banged the fuselage as the plane fell through a pocket of turbulence. He was aware of the commotion around him, but his eyes were on the forest below as the plane banked in its search for a place to set down. He thought of how much the treetops resembled the cloud tops they had passed through and how he was going to die when he reached them. He caught a brief glimpse of the river and kept its image in his mind after the plane had leveled off, how beautiful it was and how he was going to be a part of it. He was terrified but his terror was like his vision of the river, brief and remote and shining. He heard gongs, and then he became a gong and a scream of tearing metal.

When he regained consciousness, he was first aware of warmth and a peculiar and pungent smell of pig grease and herbs. His head was cradled by an arm, and he swallowed a warm fluid. Then he realized that he had the nipple of a woman's breast in his mouth, that he was, in fact, being suckled. He was too weak to resist, and as he became inured to the odor of the body he began to enjoy it. He wasn't sure where he was or who he was and for a time, independently of the People, believed he had been born again.

During the period of Russell's recovery, which seemed to take months, Kopa ki brought him food and water and kept the curious of his tribe at bay. At night, the mosquitos were murderous, and Russell slept wrapped in a parachute Kopa ki brought him. He suffered periodic malaria attacks and would again lose track of the passing time during his comatose fevers. Malaria was as normal and regular an occurrence to the People as menstruation. When it killed someone, it was because a jealous ancestor had come for them, and within a few days their bones hung in a bag on a wall of the house in which they had lived.

Kopa ki brought Russell water and sweet potatoes and starchy cakes of taro. He brought meat, and Russell ate it. Later he wondered if it had been pork or human meat, but he didn't ask. Kopa ki brought him medicines he had found in the wreckage of the plane, and Russell took quinine in the doses he remembered the army medics administering. When he was well enough to join in the life of the village, he was taken to the house of the men and shown the eight-foot bamboo flutes the women were never permitted to see but which, when heard, drove them into a sexual frenzy. He feasted with the men on wild pig, but when they took a prisoner from another tribe or brought back a dead warrior and roasted him on a spit or baked him in clay, Russell refused the choice parts offered him.

"Where I come from," Russell explained to Kopa ki, "it is forbidden to eat the meat of men."

"But it is the best." Kopa ki shook his head in dismay. He was relishing what appeared to be a human forearm. "I hope the land to which I must go is not where you come from. It is a great joy to eat one's enemies."

13

SOMETIMES WEEKS WOULD GO BY without Russell's giving a thought to the spot near the corner of Ottawa and Main, a spot he passed almost every day on his way to the office, where his great-grandfather had been hanged.

According to J.M. Leet's *Early Days of Wing County* (set down in green buckram on typed onionskin), Ambrose Wheeler had been strung up by an angry mob on a raw October evening in 1880 for a murder he didn't commit. It had been a shameful episode for the settlers and their immediate issue, but the passing of a century made it a legend, a distinction comparable to Green Castle, Indiana's veiled pride in having a bank once robbed by John Dillinger.

Russell held no grudge against the people of Five Oaks. As a boy, when he and his buddies had played at being the Youngers or the James Gang, he'd enjoyed being able to say that his own great-grandfather had been the last man known to have been hanged in the county. It had given his outlawry a halo of authenticity. Later, as the town's largest employer, it provided a common touch.

According to Russell's father, Daniel, Great-Granddaddy Ambrose had probably needed hanging, if not for the murder of his mistress, Mrs. Tredwell Johnston, then for an accumulation of transgressions going back to his days as a captain in Wesley Merritt's cavalry, harrassing Mosby's Confederacy east of the Shenandoah Valley.

In fighting Mosby's raiders, it was said that Ambrose had become so adept as a guerrilla fighter that he'd continued his forays on the defeated South long after Appomattox, and become wealthy in the process. How else could he have lived the way he did, built his big house, gambled, whored and become creditor (so the family believed, though Leet didn't mention it), to half the crowd who lynched him? He had come home almost a year later than the other men of Five Oaks with a chestful of medals, and had done little to dispel stories that he had personally killed over a hundred Confederates and that his company had taken no prisoners.

The lynch mob, led by Tredwell Johnston himself, took its revenge fifteen years after the war when the luster on Ambrose's medals had tarnished. The resentment of those veterans who had fought with small glory in the 5th Michigan Infantry had been inflamed by gambling debts owed Ambrose, and they conveniently rekindled their ire with the conviction that he had not fought out of any sense of patriotism or for the preservation of the Union, but purely for adventure and profit. The real killer was apprehended a week later when he tried to pawn off a gold brooch on Johnny Puff, a whoring buddy of Ambrose's. The brooch was known by Puff to have been given to Pauline Johnston by Ambrose himself. Mr. Johnston, doubly grieved, apologized to the Widow Wheeler and her infant son, Cyrus, on behalf of the people of Five Oaks. They gave her the brooch and $230 in gold and called it even.

Russell often wondered how this supposedly desperate character had fathered a line of stolid businessmen, so-called pillars of the community. Had the family unconsciously (or consciously) been trying to atone for this aberration in its heritage? Or had Ambrose simply been given as bad a rap on his whole life story as on the episode which had brought it to an early end? Russell wondered if there were any living descendants of Jesse James and, if so, how they now regarded their notorious ancestor.

Obviously there had been some basis for the town's feelings about Ambrose in those years following the Civil War. Russell had evidence of this in Ambrose's pistol, an 1851, .36 caliber Colt Navy, on the butt of which there were six carved notches. That the pistol had been handed down to Russell through three generations suggested that Ambrose's memory had been considered worth preserving. The pistol had come into Russell's hands when his grandfather died. His father apparently hadn't cared about possessing it. Russell didn't know why, and he wondered at what point he would pass on to Nick this tainted Excaliber of the Wheeler succession. Considering the lackluster lives which had followed Ambrose's, his was a myth worth fostering.

Occasionally Russell took the revolver down from its dark perch above the cornice of his den wall. He would appreciate the surprising heft of it, half cock it and savor the click of the spinning cylinder, full cock it and aim through the sight on the lip of the hammer and then ease back the spring. Finally he would contemplate the six crudely carved notches in the handle, now whitening with age and with the residue of brass polish he used on the backstrap. There was a story there, or six stories. Of course it was possible that Ambrose had never shot anyone, that he had notched his pistol purely for effect, though Russell doubted it when he considered the authenticity of the rope stretched out by the weight of his great-grandfather's body.

14

T HE WORLD IN WHICH NICK grew up was vastly different from that Russell had known, not only in the particulars
of history but because of the extra scrutiny he received as
his father's son. Once thing he didn't want to be was a businessman. His father had to wear a suit every day and sit in
an office for longer than Nick had to stay in school. From a
child's-eye view, the world was full of possibilities, and his
idea of what he would become changed as frequently as the
Friday night movie at the Odeon Theater. The week after
seeing John Wayne in *The Wake of the Red Witch* he was set
on becoming captain of a sailing ship. Before that he'd
wanted to be a hobo. For several Saturdays after he'd seen a
film about men who lived on the rails, he left home with a
Spam sandwich in a paper bag, a compass and a ball of
twine (though he wasn't sure why he included the twine).
He walked north several blocks to the edge of town, then
cut across a rolling field to a grassy bank overlooking the
railroad tracks where he lay in a profound air of freedom
and tallied all the routines by which he would no longer be
bound. No more school, no more Cub Scouts, no more
Sunday school, no more baths and wearing suits and having
to be polite on Thanksgiving Day at his grandmother's or
New Year's Day at the country club near Grand Rapids to
which his parents belonged. A new life was churning its
way down the rails. A perpetual summer approached.

This delirious emancipation lasted until the train passed
below the bank and disappeared around the long curve to
the west. As it roared and clattered below him, he tried to

imagine leaping to the roof of one of the box cars, grabbing the rung of a ladder or finding a handhold in an open door and pulling himself up. But the clanking of the cars was so much louder and the grinding of the wheels so much more menacing than those of the trains in the movies. And as the ground shuddered under his feet and cinders flew in the light spring air, he clutched handfuls of field grass as one might the mane of a galloping horse and relished nestling close to the unmoving earth. He listened as the horn moaned its way to the west, and when he had finished his sandwich and consulted his compass, he walked back towards town.

After school Nick would come home and wander through his father's house. He looked at the pictures of the sailing ships on the storm-tossed seas which adorned the living room walls. He gazed at the picture window without seeing the garden beyond it and felt the loneliness in the dust-filled sunlight streaming in over the sofa, casting rainbow fragments from the prism lamps on the table. He read the titles on the yellow and green spines of the books on the shelves and wondered about the real life that was out there where he had never been.

Occasionally, when he had explored some possible future as far as his imagination would take him, he would announce his plan to test the kind of response it would get. Being a cowboy, he decided, would be as good as being a hobo, and the clothes were neater. But he wondered how you went about becoming one.

"That's something to dream about," his father said as he carved a slice off the roast and forked it onto the first of the four plates stacked before him.

"Well, that's what I'm gonna be," Nick insisted.

"You'll have to go to cowboy school," Marlis teased.

"Where's that?"

"Oh, that comes after high school, if you can get in. And then you have to go to cowboy college." She winked at her father.

Nick looked deflated. He'd just come in from a gun fight with Donnie Slocum, and he fingered his cap pistol in its holster under the table.

"Marlis is just having fun." His mother reached over and brushed a few stray hairs off his forehead.

"Is that right, Dad?"

"There's no cowboy college," Russell said wearily. He set the last plate with its desiccated slice of pot roast in front of Nick. "In fact, there aren't any cowboys anymore."

"The Durango Kid's a cowboy," Nick countered.

"That's just in the movies." Russell took the mashed potatoes from Marlis, scooped up a large spoonful and shook it vigorously at his plate. "Besides, if he was real, he'd get powder burns from resting the barrel of his pistol on his forearm when he shoots. Those guys are just make believe."

"That's not true! Donnie Slocum saw Gene Autry in person."

Before he'd come home, Russell had had a long argument with Paul Blakely about whether or not they were ready to go into production with their padded mailing bags, and he was not in a mood to argue with a ten-year-old. He reached over and pinched Nick's shoulder. "Gene Autry is just in the movies. There are no cowboys, understand? And I don't like being contradicted."

"You'd better apologize," Miriam said.

"Huh?"

"Tell your father you're sorry."

"What for?"

"Don't be rude." She glared at him. "I won't have a rude son. You say I'm sorry right now."

"But what did I do?"

"Nick . . ." It was the look in Russell's eyes as much as the timbre of his voice that told Nick there would be no further explanation.

"I'm sorry," Nick whispered.

"I couldn't hear you," his father intoned.

"I'm sorry."

When he'd been excused from the table, Nick went to his room, took off his gunbelt, wrapped it around the holster and put it in the cardboard box under his bed with his three-wheeled truck and his torn drum.

15

Because she admired him, Marlis often tried to be like her father. As a child she imitated his mannerisms, his posture, his way of walking, and Russell found this charming. But as she passed adolescence, it began to annoy him, and he regarded his irritation as a failing in himself, a defect of love. "Well, look at it this way," she might say in the course of a discussion, as she leaned back in her chair and stared portentiously at the ceiling.

Russell would take a deep breath to contain his impatience. Oh my God get to the point, he would think to himself. Would you please just say it, or shut up.

When he was away on business and feeling nostalgic, he thought of her fondly, and when talk of children came up, he would pass around her photograph, along with Nick's, and say, "I don't worry about Marlis. She's got her head screwed on right."

But he did worry about Marlis. She was willful like her mother, and he was afraid she might "get in trouble," as was said of girls who mysteriously left school to live with an aunt in a neighboring state or to marry the teenage father of their expected child. In Five Oaks, such marriages seemed more the rule than the exception, and the aphorism, often repeated in the local taverns and barbershops, was that you wouldn't buy a pair of shoes without trying them on.

Russell sometimes wondered about the feelings of men he knew whose daughters prematurely became mothers. Did they feel they had failed?

Buck Leech's daughter, Kristy, had had to marry Jim Pressler, son of the second shift maintenance foreman at the mill. Pressler was a nice enough boy, but Russell wondered how long it could last. What would Buck and Laura and the elder Presslers talk about? He wondered if he was becoming a snob. No, it isn't that, he assured himself. Laura had arranged the wedding on two week's notice. Buck had given his daughter away and thrown a sizeable reception at the Five Oaks Country Club. To all observers it was a joyous occasion. Privately, Buck joked about white shotguns.

"It's so sad," Miriam sighed.

"Maybe it'll be just fine." Russell tried to assuage her.

"Don't be absurd," she fumed. "All their plans, ruined."

"Whose plans?"

She glared at him for being willfully obtuse.

Kristy had asked Marlis to be her maid-of-honor. At first Miriam had objected, but finally she decided it wouldn't be worth a major row.

"Do you think I might be tainted by association?" Marlis taunted.

"No dear."

"Do you think it'll make me a party to the scandal?"

"No. It's just that . . ."

"Just what?"

"I won't have you talking to me this way."

"Oh, go to hell!" Marlis stomped up the stairs, and the slamming of her bedroom door boomed through the house.

Russell waited five minutes before going up to talk to her. He cleared his throat to announce his presence. "I think you owe your mother an apology," he said.

"But she's such a hypocrite, Dad."

"Marlis!"

"Well, she is."

"She's just worried about you. It's only natural."

"You don't have to worry about me, Dad. I'm not going to get knocked up by anybody in this hick town."

"This hick town?"

"Oh, you know what I mean."

"I'm not sure I do."

"People here are just so limited. They don't know about anything but Five Oaks."

"And what do you know?"

"I know I don't want to live here."

"Where do you want to live?"

"New York maybe. Or Florence, or Vienna."

"Why Vienna?"

"Oh I don't know. That's just a for-instance. It could be Byzantium. I just know I'm not going to end up wasting away with some farmer or pulp cutter in Five Oaks, that's all."

"Well, it's your life." Russell felt a bit dazed, as he often did when talking with Marlis. He caught himself again wishing that she might be a bit more feminine, a bit more pliant. Then he remembered why he had come to her room. "But would you please apologize to your mother?"

"I don't have to apologize."

"I know you don't have to. But wouldn't you do it for me? As a favor? Please?"

"Well, okay. As a favor. But I won't mean it."

Russell kissed her on the forehead, then turned and walked downstairs, picked up his briefcase and left for the office.

16

ONE NIGHT WHEN MARLIS WAS FOURTEEN and had been unable to fall asleep, she sat up in bed to look at the luminous dial of the electric clock on her desk and was surprised to discover that there was no light whatsoever in her room. She switched on the lamp on the nightstand by her bed and saw that the hands of the clock rested at 8:15. But it couldn't be 8:15, she reasoned. It had been almost 11:00 when she had gone to bed, and if it were 8:15 in the morning, there would be daylight coming through the windows and she would be late for school. Then she remembered that her father was away on business and she had borrowed his electric razor to shave the fuzz that had begun to become noticable on her shins. Because she had been listening to her LP of *Kismet*, she had unplugged the clock in order to plug in the razor.

She got out of bed and reconnected the clock to the wall socket under her desk. But what time is it now, she mused? She looked at the telephone and wondered if the operator would be angry if she called for the time so late at night. But when she lifted the reciever, she heard a man's voice on the line. It was a voice she had heard before, though she couldn't think where.

". . . No good reason you can't get away if you want to. It's been a month. More than a month."

"Wait a minute, Dwight," her mother's voice broke in, "there's somebody on the line. Who's there? Who's on this line?"

"Hello," Marlis said. "I was trying to get the operator."

"What the hell for, at this time of night?" Marlis was startled by her mother's tone of voice.

"I needed to know what time it is. My clock got unplugged."

"It's 12:30. Now get off the line! No, wait a minute. Say hello to Dr. Sanders. He called to tell me about an old friend who's been ill." Her mother's voice became more measured. "Dr. Sanders, this is my daughter Marlis."

"Hello Marlis. Your mother's told me so much about you."

"Hello." Marlis spoke tentatively. She knew that voice; she was sure.

"I'm afraid I called rather late," the voice said. "But I had some important news for your mother about her friend."

Called rather late, Marlis thought. She hadn't heard the phone ring. There was something about the way he said "rather," as if it rhymed with "bother." Then she remembered where she had heard the voice before.

"Now go back to bed Marlis, it's a school night." Her mother's voice affected sweetness.

"Good night Marlis," the man said. "It was nice talking with you."

Marlis put the receiver back in the cradle and sat looking at its heavy black shape. It seemed predatory. Rings of light filled the air around it, and she wondered if her mother and the man might still be talking.

Carlson! That was the name. She remembered slicked-down hair, a dark complexion and the beautifully tailored suit of the man in the hallway in Detroit the previous summer. Miriam had taken her to spend the night at the Ponchartrain Hotel and to shop for school clothes at Hudson's. She'd ordered room service for Marlis and told her she was going out to have dinner with a cousin whom she hadn't seen in years. It had gotten late. The last movie on the television had turned to snow, and Marlis was wondering what might be keeping Miriam when she heard voices in the hall. She tiptoed to the door and listened to her mother's voice and the voice of a man. They were muffled, breathless. Marlis was afraid someone might be attacking her mother and opened the door to see.

"Oh Marlis!" Her mother stood facing the man. "You frightened me. We didn't want to wake you." Miriam looked flushed, as if she might have been running. "Marlis, this is, umm, Mr. Carlson. John Carlson. Mr. Carlson is married to my cousin Mary. He was kind enough to see me home."

"Hello, Marlis. I didn't think I'd get to meet you. It's *raaather* late."

"Thank you, John." Her mother extended her hand to the man, and he took it uncertainly.

"Miriam." He sounded as if he were about to ask her a question.

"Please thank Mary again. I had a lovely time."

"I will. Yes," the man said. "I'll do that. Goodnight."

Her mother guided Marlis back into the the room, closed the door behind them and fastened the nightchain. "We had a lovely dinner," she said. "I hadn't seen Mary in years and years."

"Mary?" Marlis inquired.

"You wouldn't remember her, dear." Miriam stood in front of the mirror, removing her earrings. "Your father isn't fond of Mary for some reason. In fact he doesn't like her very much, I'm afraid. That's why I haven't seen her for so many years. I think it would be best if we didn't say anything about my having seen her. Okay? I know I can count on you to keep a secret."

MARLIS STILL HADN'T RESET the clock. What time is it now, she wondered. Her mother had said 12:30. The dial cast a green light over her desk. One o'clock, she thought. Maybe. She set the hour hand at one. In any case, it's late, she thought, really *raaather* late.

17

ONE EVENING IN 1958, RUSSELL came home to discover that Miriam had gone to bed with a headache. It seemed curious that she had contracted a headache on a Friday evening on which they had nothing planned. It wouldn't have been unusual if they had been invited to a party or were having company for dinner. Miriam was frequently stricken with a convenient malaise, leaving Russell to entertain their guests alone.

"Miriam isn't feeling well," had become a cliché Russell blushed to repeat. He swallowed the words as he spoke. His eyes would momentarily beg for understanding and then glaze over to indicate he would entertain no more discussion of Miriam's absence or the reasons for it.

It might be the wife of a regional sales manager, on a visit to the home office with her husband, a distributor or the president of a large chain of office supply stores. It didn't matter. Miriam's reluctance to receive them and the apologies for her absence were indiscriminate.

"She wanted me to be sure and tell you how sorry she is to miss seeing you. What can I get you to drink?"

Josephine served dinner and Russell entertained like a seasoned bachelor. Miriam planned everything: the wine, the china, the crystal, the seating arrangements. She would allow those people she couldn't bring herself to see no opportunity to fault her skills as a hostess. And on those rare occasions when she did make herself available, she could be charming. She could make her guests feel like visiting royalty, make them feel privileged to be in her company. Though frequently after a third bottle of wine or with the stingers and rusty nails which followed dessert she would become a little too charming. She might improvise a rumba as she rose from the table, become unflatteringly frank or lapse into one of her Mae West routines. "Why don't you come up and see me sometime?" Miriam would roll her eyes suggestively and bump a shapely hip at an unassuming executive, struggling under his collar to find a proper balance between congeniality and decorum. "Peel me a grape," she might say.

Once Russell watched helplessly as she sidled up to the vice president of a Chicago bank and said, "Is that a pickle in your pocket or are you just glad to see me?"

Another night after Miriam had attacked Gale Putney for her use of the word "folks" when she meant "people," her organizing of "coffee klatsches" and the "unbelievable homeliness" of her dress, she turned and fled up the stairs in a rage. Russell followed her up to their bedroom.

"I feel sorry for you," he said. "I really do."

"Oh keep it," she snarled. She threw herself on the bed and turned away from him, clutching a pillow in her arms. "Goddamn you."

"I'm telling you, Miriam. I know you don't want to hear it, but you need help. You can't treat people that way."

"To hell with them. And to hell with you and your goddamned precious company, your boring little town and your fuddy-duddy friends."

"This company," Russell tried to speak calmly, "provides you all these things you care so much about. And it's your town, too. You grew up here."

"Well, I wouldn't be stuck in it if it wasn't for you."

"I feel sorry for you, Miriam. That's all I can say."

"Oh goddamn you," she yelled. "Goddamn your big stupid superior you." She pounded the mattress with her fist and her shoulders began convulsing. He covered her with a blanket but she threw it off instantly. She shrieked, and her anger exploded in a flurry of kicks on the bedspread.

Russell turned to go back to face the guests he'd left in

stunned silence. He opened the bedroom door and almost tripped over something in the hall.

"Nick?" The pajama-clad body was huddled in a fetal ball at his feet.

"What's wrong with Mommy?" Nick's words came in half-suppressed sobs.

Russell reached down and lifted Nick in his arms. "Mommy hurt herself," he said. "She fell down and hurt herself. She just wants to be alone right now."

NICK REMEMBERED LYING IN BED another night, hearing the music and laughter seep under the door of his room along with the light from the hall. Marlis had gone out on a date, and he had eaten alone in the kitchen with Josephine. She had let him watch television in the den while she served dinner to the adults, and later she took him upstairs and heard his prayers. Nick lay in bed thinking about the blond woman on *Your Hit Parade* who sang "Shrimp Boats is a' Comin'." The words of the refrain, "Why don't you hurry, hurry, hurry home. Why don't you hurry, hurry, hurry home," ran through his mind again and again, like a Möbius strip. He was thinking that his head might burst if he couldn't stop the song when the door to his bedroom opened suddenly. A shadow stood against the light from the hall. The music in his head gave way to the music from the party downstairs, and he recognized the silhouette as that of his mother, the cinched waist of her dress, the hair wound tightly to her head, the dangling earrings. She stepped sideways, then came toward him, then sideways again as if on a ship in a stormy sea.

"Nicky, it's Mommy," Miriam whispered hoarsely. She lurched against the bed, sat down and reached out for him. "Nicky, Nicky, Nicky." She slurred his name, and her hands groped for him through the bedcovers. Her breath had a sour smell, and he tried to pull away. "What's a matter, Nicky? It's Mommy. Don't you love Mommy?" The shadow resembled his mother but it frightened him. She was clutching at his neck and shoulders. He slid back on his pillow until he felt the turnings of the headboard pressing into his back.

"Don't Nicky. Don't," the voice pleaded. "I need you Nicky. You're the only one who loves me."

"No," Nick cried. "Go away." The hands kept grasping, and he tried to push them from him. Suddenly there was a flash of light. He felt the sting across his face and the bite of her ring on his ear.

The voice changed. "You little bastard. You don't love me. After all I've done for you."

"No, no," Nick cried. He thought it might be a dream. This couldn't be his mother. Another hand reached out and grabbed his face.

"Maybe you won't have a mother someday. Won't you be sorry then. Little Nicky won't have a mother and he'll wish he'd loved her."

"No," he cried again. "No Mom, don't!"

"Oh no," she muttered. The shadow rose from his bed and staggered back toward the door. "Oh no. You'll be a sorry little boy. You'll see." She bumped against the door-jamb and into the hall. The door slammed behind her.

Nick sat pressed against the headboard, thinking through the muffled music and laughter, watching the crack of light under the door.

MAYBE IT WAS THE DRIVE, Russell thought. You get all tensed up, and it feels like your head's coming off. He was thinking of reasons why Miriam might've gone to bed with a headache on an evening on which she had no obligations to escape. It was Josephine's night off, and Miriam had just returned from a three-day trip to Chicago. Russell had been fantasizing about their reunion when he arrived home to find the house quiet and her note on the kitchen desk. *Gone to bed. Bad headache. Chicken pot pie in the oven.*

Nick was spending the night at Donnie Slocum's, and Marlis came home from the movies with a gangling boy she didn't bother to introduce. She would soon be eighteen, and Russell had begun to notice how her hips had begun to move with a purposeful fluidity. Even in a loose-fitting blouse her breasts were prominent. And there was something in her eyes that brought him up short, an unmistakable assurance he remembered in Miriam, and he knew that whatever might be happening down in the basement rec room would be precisely what Marlis wanted to happen. Miriam had lost that look. Or maybe she had simply lost her desire.

He recalled a portrait of his mother, one he had discovered only a few years earlier while sorting through his father's effects, and how it had perplexed him. Because of the curve of her cheekbones and her high, broad forehead, the girl in sepia was clearly his mother, probably in her late teens, but the look in her eyes had a longing, palpably sexual quality he couldn't correlate with the bovine Victorian woman he remembered. In the week following his father's funeral he found the photograph in a drawer of his father's night table and with it his first inkling of the quality of attraction she might have once held. In Russell's memories, his mother had all the spontaneity and amatory appeal of a clam, and when he thought of her it wasn't the woman who came to mind so much as her aphorisms: *The tree is known by its fruit; Where your treasure is there will your heart be also; Lust is bait for the devil's trap.*

Lust is bait for the marriage bed, he thought.

It had been two hours and ten minutes since Marlis had led her date down the basement stairs. Russell could hear the mellifluous crooning of Johnny Mathis. "Excellent make-out music," Marlis had called it, and he wondered what her definition of "making-out" might include.

He walked from the den to the kitchen, ostensibly for a snack or something to drink, though he wanted nothing. He lingered at the head of the stairs but heard only singing and violins, no talking, no laughter, no reassuring clatter of pool balls. He wondered if he ought to make some excuse to go down and investigate, say he was checking the furnace. But it was a warm spring night, and the furnace was cold. He wondered if he was being a good father.

Miriam's trips to Detroit and Chicago had become fairly regular, once or twice a month. She had said this one was to see an Impressionist exhibit at the Art Institute and to do some shopping. Russell knew Miriam was bored but not what to do about it. Her daily activities were a mystery. She seldom participated in the social life of Five Oaks. She told Russell she felt on display, felt she was always being judged. And the less frequently she appeared, the more threatening the idea of an appearance became.

Russell ascribed Miriam's reclusive behavior largely to her drinking. She had distanced herself from everyone she had known, and her girlhood friends had become curious strangers. Or was her drinking only a symptom? She had become a conversation piece in her seclusion, and an embarrassment when she did venture out in her alcoholic veil. She found it easier to create another life for herself in distant and not-so-distant cities and made the hour-and-a-half drive to Grand Rapids at least once a week. She had friends there, some of whom he knew and some who were only names to him. One of these was a woman named Elaine who faced frequent crises.

"Elaine's having a bad night. I'm going to stay with her," said a typical message left for him with Josephine.

To Marlis, Elaine had become a tiresome joke. "Oh, is Elaine dying again?" she would say, noting her mother's vacant place at the table.

"Maybe she is." Russell refused to indulge her sarcasm.

"Oh Dad, get serious. Have you ever met this Elaine person?"

"No I haven't."

"I mean you don't really believe . . ."

"Marlis! That's enough! Do you understand?"

"No I don't!"

"Pardon me?" There was an edge of a threat in Russell's voice.

"No, I don't understand Elaine, and I don't understand your putting up with it. But I do understand that we aren't going to talk about it. Right?"

"Right."

Occasionally Miriam traveled with him when he went to New York or Seattle or San Francisco on business, and to Russell those trips comprised their happiest times together. She was charming with his associates and their wives while dining at Pavillon or dancing at the Stork Club, and she rarely got drunk. She relished the theater and the celebrites they met and particularly enjoyed the company of David Gould, the account executive who handled Wheeler's advertising, and of his wife, Lucille. Each time Miriam accompanied Russell it seemed for a time that they could, after all, be happy together. But a few days after their return to Five Oaks, when she had told Marlis and Nick every detail of the shows they'd seen and the people they'd met, the glow began to fade. She tried to prolong it by singing along with the recordings of *South Pacific*, *Call Me Madam* or *West Side Story*, but the songs soon became empty reminders.

RUSSELL TURNED AWAY from the stairs and walked back to the den. Whatever was going on in the basement would go on just as easily somewhere else. Better there than in a car on some back road or on a grassy bank under the moon where anything could happen.

He sat down and poured coffee from the thermos. He spread the evening paper out over the green blotter on his desk and read about an eighteen-year-old from Nebraska who had kidnapped a fifteen-year-old girl, stolen a car and gone on a killing spree across three states. Starkweather. The name seemed chillingly correct. He thought of the prairie land where Boy Wheeler lived. Starkweather. He wondered what could cause someone to become so indifferent to life, or if people like that were simply killers from birth.

18

AFTER RUSSELL TOOK THE BLUEGILL off Katy's hook, he threaded the aluminum point of the stringer through its gill and dropped it over the gunwale with the half-dozen or so they had already caught.

"Do they like each other down there?" Katy asked.

"Down where?" Russell was poking around in the plastic cottage cheese container for another worm.

"Down there." She pointed to where the stringer of fish had just sunk below the surface.

"Well, I don't know." Russell concentrated on working the hook through the length of the worm. "It's something that hadn't occurred to me. I suppose they do, sort of. I don't know if liking each other is something fish give very much thought to."

"Why not?"

"It's just the way fish are."

"You mean they're not really friends?"

"They might be friends, I guess. They're all in the same predicament."

"What's a predicament?"

"It means they've all got the same problem, which is that they've all been caught."

"Do they know we're going to eat them?"

"No, I don't think they do."

"Oh, I'm glad," Katy sighed. She dropped her hook back in the water and resumed her vigil on the bobber.

In the brief interval that followed, each sound of nature became distinct and amplified. The manic yammering of a flicker and the *ma-lank* of a jay became other forms of silence, and a whiffling breeze stirred the paling leaves along the shore. *By this heat and this rustle I am absolved from all obligation to the past*, Russell mused on Thoreau. He felt his head snap, as if he had nodded off and then suddenly lurched back into consciousness. The shadow of a heron crossed his line. For an instant, he had a feeling someone else was in the boat with him, someone other than Katy, and he shot a glance at the empty seat to his left. He smelled sunlight, the warmth of the sun on Lesley's hair. She had been working in her garden when he'd arrived to pick up Katy, and when she'd hugged him he'd felt the heat of the sun in his arms and smelled the redolence of it when he'd kissed her hair. He closed his eyes now and inhaled, feeling the warmth of her body again and imagining the dampness his shirt had absorbed. She was wearing khaki shorts and a yellow halter top, and his hands had come to rest on her bare midriff. His hands were slipping in the perspiration on her back now, slipping over the points of her hips, his fingers tracing her sacral dimples and then cupping the moist fullness of her buttocks, the silk of her panties caressing his knuckles as she pressed her pelvis into him.

Russell's head snapped again. He straightened and glanced at Katy as a crow called over the water. Now, he thought, now. Here and now. He pulled his line up to see if he still had a worm on. He did. He leaned over to watch it sink again, but his gaze was arrested at the surface by a gray-haired man whose head bulged and contracted in the ripples stirred by his rocking of the boat. His friend, Kopa ki, had believed a man's reflection was the face of his spirit, that it dwelled in the depths and rose to remind him of his origin. Kopa ki, Kopa ki, Kopa ki. Russell ran the name over and over in his mind and thought how appropriately the sound of it suited the playfulness of the man.

Kopa ki had taken him to a well worn spot on a ridge overlooking the escarpment of the river. Here he called out to the valley, then rose on his toes in anticipation, and when his voice came back to him, he turned to Russell.

"Listen," he said. He stood proudly as if he were receiving great praise.

"What is it?" Russell wondered what Kopa ki made of the echo.

"It is the voice of my spirit from the river," Kopa ki answered.

"And what does your spirit say?" Russell asked.

"It tells me that I am still with the living." Kopa ki nodded profoundly and rhythmically. "That I have not yet been taken by my ancestors."

He told Russell of a deep pool called Raunwara, high in the mountains. "It is from this pool that the first people came. It is the source of my ancestors and of the river."

Kopa ki's lithe build made him seem tall, and in a world without Russell's frame of reference, he was a tall man. It was only when Russell regained enough strength to stand that Kopa ki shrank to barely the height of his shoulder.

Russell had no idea how long he had been among the People. A year, two years? His periodic bouts with malaria kept him from any accurate count of the days, and the People had no calendar. To them time meant birth, puberty, and death. They kept no count of the rising and setting of the sun and the phases of the moon. He knew only that he had been with them long enough to notice the body of Kopa ki's son, Ring du, thickening and becoming that of a man.

When the time came for the initiation of the village boys into the mysteries of manhood, Kopa ki invited Russell to attend. There was a long house in the village which woman and children were forbidden to enter. It was the house of the men, in which were kept the great birds which brought fertility to the People. The mournful song of the birds which aroused the women came from this house, and they knew that if they should see the birds that brought life, it would bring them certain death.

Ring du and the other boys his age were taken into the house. They had spent one last night with their mothers as children and would never be their mother's children again.

If they survived the ceremony, they were told, they would emerge as men.

The boys were seated in a circle around a fire pit and kept awake without food or water for three nights and three days. At the first sign of drowsiness, they heard a great rustling of leaves, and monsters appeared with huge moon-shaped heads of clay and threatened them with axes and knives held to their throats. All the while the great birds sang their deep mournful song. By the end of the three days the boys were mildly delirious. They had forgotten their childhoods, Kopa ki explained, and were ready to be men.

Now the secret of the great birds was revealed to the boys, the great birds which were forbidden to the sight of the women and children. And the secret was this: that there were no great birds, that the power to give birth to men had once belonged to the women, but that the men had stolen it away from them. The great birds were in fact enormous flutes, some eight feet long, and their mournful song was the breath of the men blowing through them. Now the boys knew the secret power the men had over the stupid women and children, and they were threatened again with the knives and axes. If they spoke of this to any woman or uninitiated male, they would be killed and the power of fertility would leave the People, and the People would die and be no more, and their souls would be eaten by the true great birds that dwelled in the land of the dead.

When the boys had been sufficiently frightened and impressed, they were circumcised, doused with the bright red oil of pressed pandamus seeds which symbolized the blood of birth, and then carried out through the village with much shouting. The elders proclaimed, "Here is a newborn man, an independent man. He must be treated as a man. He must never again be a child. We, the men, have given birth to him."

Russell wondered if there was some ritual he had neglected with Nick, some revelation of secrets that he had failed to pass on. Perhaps civilization had lost this to progress and practicality. If there were secrets he didn't know them. Or was the true revelation simply that there were no secrets, nothing to rely on but one's own best effort? Nick might've believed that, Russell thought, if I hadn't been so lucky.

But luck had clouded the picture.

"HEY GAMPS."

Russell was roused when Katy shrieked that she had another fish on the line. He watched her bring it in. She lay the rod on the floor of the boat, straddled the tip, and pulled the line in by hand. She had hooked a bullhead, larger than any of the bluegills they had caught, and as she brought it to the surface, the fish jumped and startled her so that she dropped the line and had to pull it in all over again.

"Holy cow," Katy yelled. "It's a monster."

This time Russell helped her. He lifted the bullhead by the leader and laid it on the floor of the boat between them.

"Ouuh, it's so ugly," Katy squealed.

"It is," Russell laughed. "A face only another bullhead could love."

"This one's for Mom," Katy giggled. She pressed her hands together with excitement. "She'll be scared."

Russell slid his hand down over the fish's head, being careful to compress its spiney dorsal fin. "I think we've got all we need to impress your mother," Russell said. He worked the hook free and laid the bullhead in the bilge. He pulled in the stringer of bluegills, then turned and took up the oars and began rowing back to the dock.

By now, the People were probably civilized, Russell thought. The gods of the sky would have brought them all the amazing things first given the white man. They would no longer eat their enemies or bury babies or fear the dead. The men would no longer give birth to their sons, and they would not be the People anymore. Kopa ki's infant son, Matu, might still be living, an old man of forty-five, carrying sap on a rubber plantation. He would wear no tusks on his arm, and his son, in turn, would be a white-shirted clerk selling souvenir carvings in Port Moresby.

19

Russell enjoyed feeling the late afternoon sun as he sat at his desk reading a book called *Nature's Diary*. He found himself hunting in the taiga of central Russia, observing that fine edge where the life of a man comes up against all that is untamed in him, where the first bare ground of spring is greeted with the astonishment of a weary explorer discovering a new continent. It was a wilder reflection of the delight he had known as a boy, hunting first with his father and then alone, not so much hunting as becoming absorbed in the life of his prey, beginning to see through the eye of a deer or a grouse.

"It is my jubilee year," wrote Mikhael Prishvin, who had been born the same year as Russell's grandfather, "and I will write no fiction but put everything down without changing the names even, and record each day of the spring. Let the earth itself be the hero of my story."

Russell felt the sun spreading through his head like water through a dry sponge and imagined his brain beginning to bake, to ferment, becoming a different kind of brain, capable of perceptions as yet unknown. His jubilee year had long passed, but maybe it still wasn't too late to give himself over to pure observation. He would disconnect the phone, ignore the mail, turn all his affairs over to his attorneys. He would set the company and the community free to survive without him, as they would have to do one day in any case. Everyone should have the opportunity to live untrammelled at least one year before their death, to die to the world and yet stay in it, without identity, without demands of or from it, a year of living as if before birth or after death, to see everything and be seen by nothing.

There was a breeze over the lake, and from the fine ripples on its surface, the sunlight cast a meteor shower on the ceiling over his head, shimmering as if the house itself were a living thing.

I stood there leaning on my spade thrust deep in the snow, my heart brimming with love—but for whom, I could not tell. Here was a Thoreau with even more joy and humor. I want to be drunk and own nothing, Russell thought. I want to sleep in the nest of a wood duck and never comb my hair.

He thought back over his trip to Pine Ridge with Boy and how deeply affected he had been by the dancing, watching mechanics and farmers and seamstresses named Frank or Dennis or Wanda, ordinary lives lived in reverence for the land in the spirit of their ancestors. The children in their beaded leggings and bustles of eagle feathers had especially moved him, because they were not children in costumes but actual Indians, absorbed in the drums and the wailing of the singers, becoming the spirit of the deer or the buffalo or the grass as they danced. He thought of Kopa ki as he watched them, and when he turned back to look at Boy standing next to him, he had to wipe the tears from his cheeks.

His reverie was broken by Lily's barking. She stirred from the couch, and her toenails clicked on the hardwood floor as she trotted, growling, toward the front hall.

From the kitchen window he could see Lesley getting out of her Subaru. The annoyance he had felt at someone arriving unannounced became delight on seeing it was Lesley, and then concern as she approached the front door and he could see she'd been crying. She opened her mouth as if to speak, then fell into his arms and buried her head against his shoulder. She held onto him with what felt like desperation. Lily stopped barking; the hair along her spine lay back down as she sniffed the leg of Lesley's jeans and her tail thumped against the open door.

"Okay," Russell crooned, "sssh." He stroked Lesley's hair. "It's okay."

He walked her into the den, sat on the couch and held her across his lap. Soon she began sobbing, and though he felt the pain in her convulsions and in her small cries at his throat, he also felt a sense of completeness he hadn't known in years, his jubilee fantasies absorbed by the life in his arms. Lesley's hair cascaded over his shoulder. He moved his hand under the fall of it and massaged the back of her neck.

"Sssh," he whispered. He kissed her hair and rocked her gently. "Sssh. It's all right. Sssh. I love you, Lesley. It's all right. Sssh."

"HE LEFT A NOTE," she told him when he returned with a cup of tea. "I came home from work and found it on the kitchen table." They sat sideways, facing each other on the couch, and she held onto her teacup with both hands. "I found her letters in his desk. But I already knew. I just couldn't stand the silence anymore. I know what you're thinking," she said, "but I couldn't help it. I went on pretending it was a kind of mid-life crisis or something. But I just couldn't be closed out anymore."

Lesley dabbed her cheeks with a tissue and then blew her nose. "When he came back from Viet Nam he just didn't seem to care about things anymore. And yet he seemed to need so much love. Too much. You know how it is when someone needs too much? You dry up, like way down somewhere you want to teach them a lesson."

"Yes," Russell said. "I know."

"I'm sure that I changed too. It's just easier to see in someone else. I hated myself for feeling the way I did. I'd started casework, and I felt important to a lot of people, more than just a satellite or an auxiliary of Nick."

Russell only half-listened to what she was saying.

"I know I told you I hadn't been able to get pregnant, but that wasn't true. After Viet Nam Nick decided he didn't want any children. He said he thought it would be cruel to bring a child into this world, but I'd heard that before. I thought if he actually had a child he'd feel differently, he'd have someone else to care about. So I stopped taking the pill." Lesley paused, rubbed her eyes with her fingertips and looked out the window at the trees.

"But honestly Russ, you'd have thought I'd gotten pregnant by another man. It was as if I'd betrayed him with his own child."

Russell squeezed her shoulder.

"I don't know." She sniffled. "Maybe it was me."

"No." Russell stopped her. He held her chin gently. "It's time to be honest about this. Nick never really grew up. Maybe I never let him." He took the tea cup from her hand and set it on the table. "I didn't think of him so much as a son as I did a successor, an extra life I'd been given to play with."

"Maybe." Lesley said. "Maybe that's the way it was. But whatever you did or I did, Nick is who he is right now. It's his life, his choice."

"Of course." Russell looked down at Lily on the Navaho rug at his feet.

"He's gone to that person in New York, the one whose letters I found. Philippa. I've never known anyone named Philippa. Have you?" She smiled to keep herself from crying again. "He says she loves him just for himself. I don't quite know what that means. Do you? He's been seeing her for almost three years now." She glanced out the window and took a deep breath. "He's quit the company. I don't think he's ever coming back."

"Well I'm sorry," Russell said. "I'm sorry it came to this."

Lesley lay her hand on his face. "I've got to confess I feel relieved. I could see it coming for so long. I wanted to believe I was imagining it. I kept thinking something would happen, that everything would work out somehow."

20

T HE LONGER RUSSELL STAYED with the People the less he thought about the war, and his memories of the world that had spawned it grew more remote. The trek over Ghost Mountain had convinced him that it would be impossible to make it to the coast on his own, however far away it might be. He didn't know what he would find there anyway. Americans? Japanese? From time to time he heard distant explosions which the People regarded as thunder or the drums of unknown tribes. And once in a while he heard an airplane high above the forest canopy or saw a tiny dark spot moving above the mountains.

At first he thought about how close he really was to the world, within sight of a plane that might be flying to Port Moresby to meet a ship to Australia and another ship home. But after a year, or maybe two years, the distant droning held little portent for him anymore.

The barbarous ways of the People, though they remained barbarous, were no longer shocking to Russell. They lived in ignorance as the tribes around them lived in ignorance, as his own distant ancestors had probably lived. He despaired of trying to explain the 20th century. He had been giddy over the idea of introducing the wheel, but couldn't convince them it was anything more than a novelty. The only piece of even ground was in a valley below the village. Still, he fashioned a primitive wheel, sawing laboriously through a section of casuarina log with a saw made from a human clavicle, and fitted it to an axle of bamboo. But when he took it down to the valley to demonstrate its value, the People only laughed and rolled over and over, emulating its limited magic. Kopa ki thought it an excellent toy. He carried it up the hill, and after he let it roll down again Oganay, one of the village leaders, rolled a round stone down the hill after it and they all had a good laugh.

Russell asked Kopa ki why the garden plots were so far from the village and Kopa ki told him that after a piece of ground had given birth to one or two crops of taro, it grew old and lost its power. "The spirit of the soil moves to a place it has not been before." Kopa ki scooped up a handful of earth and sifted the chalky loam through his fingers. "It goes and hides under the grass where we have not dug and waits there for us to catch it again with new seeds."

Once Russell tried to stop the People from burying a baby with the body of its mother who had died of sorcery. Unlike those who died in battle or of disease, those whose bones and skulls adorned the walls of their former dwellings, the victims of sorcery were buried in termite mounds so that the evil that had killed them would not spread through the village. Dungtu, a village "Big Man," took the baby and held it to Russell's breast. "You have no milk for this baby," Dungtu said. "Only a mother who has milk may have this child." But there was no mother who would take the child, though there were women who would suckle pigs and women who had nursed him when he had fallen from the sky. They feared the child had been infected by the sorcery.

Russell walked away into the jungle. He heard the baby crying and then heard the crying stop suddenly as the earth was piled over it. He was filled with hatred for the People. But the hatred cooled. He realized how much of their life was dictated by the demands of survival and the dark certainties of both human and supernatural revenge, and how unchanged it was from that of their ancestors a thousand years before.

He thought of a place his father had shown him, near the mouth of the Pere Marquette River, where a band of Potawatomi had ambushed an Ottawa camp, murdered all forty-seven of its inhabitants and stuck their heads on pikes along the bank. The Place of Skulls, it came to be called. He remembered the chill slanting light through the cedars, the sound of his father's paddle pulling at the water behind him and how, as they rounded the bend, he had glanced back and believed for a moment he had seen the skulls.

He wondered what would happen to America if the Japanese and the Germans won the war, and what might happen to Japan and Germany if the Allies won. And slowly the horror of the buried baby lost some of its sting.

THE PEOPLE CALLED RUSSELL "Quari," which he learned meant "friend," their friend from the sky. He was taken into the life of the village though nothing was demanded of him. He was a guest, a charge from the gods, and as such was not permitted to participate in their wars with neighboring tribes. These wars were really ritual battles, fought with great displays of bravado and contempt. Insults were shouted and charges feigned, the combatants armed with bows and arrows, spears and bamboo knives and adorned with the plumes of egrets and birds of paradise. Some of the warriors were decorated with flowers and some with animal fur. Some wore boar tusks in their noses. Sartorial invention seemed as prominent an objective as tribal retribution. There were no generals or plans of attack. Each man was an autonomous warrior, an extemporaneous dancer and an independent trophy hunter.

Victory might be decided by a single death and the battle might easily be called on account of rain. All in all it seemed to Russell a very civilized way to make war. There was no attempt to destroy the enemy or even to devastate his commissary, only to exact a due of one or two lives to avenge a past defeat.

If possible the body of the fallen would be taken by his enemies. The head was awarded to the man who had killed him, and the tribe that had suffered the loss would retire to plan its revenge. It was an endless, revolving vendetta, practiced with the exuberance of a team sport. A man who had taken a head was allowed to wear a pig tusk bracelet on his upper arm, a way of keeping score. It reminded Russell of the miniature Japanese flags painted on the fuselages of the Navy fighter planes he had seen in Port Moresby.

Kopa ki had worn four tusk-bracelets when Russell arrived and would earn two more. He was regarded as a village Big Man and honored for his wisdom as well as his prowess with a spear. The men without tusk-bracelets usually had no wives and few possessions. They lived together in the bachelor's house. Not having killed, they hadn't established that they were men who would defend what was theirs, and the decorated warriors felt free to take from them whatever they might acquire.

MATANTE, THE WOMAN WHOSE BABY was buried with her, had appeared healthy the day before her death, though her eyes were glazed with fear. She wailed that someone had placed a spell on her, and she knew she must die. Kopa ki explained to Russell that a spell might be cast by capturing bits of a victim's feces and wrapping them up in a banana leaf. The leaf was then burned in the coals of a fire, and as the smoke rose from it, the fire would work its way back into the body from which the feces had come. Russell remembered how quickly the woman had been taken with a fever. She lay on a grass mat, moaning, the perspiration bubbling up out of her like grease from a roasting pig. In the morning she was dead.

This sorcery could not go unanswered, and once the period of mourning had passed, the investigation began. The judge was an opossum trapped from the forest. The souls of the murdered took residence in the bodies of marsupials until their deaths were avenged, Kopa ki explained. So the opossum was caged and offered bits of sweet potato. A name was chanted for each piece of sweet potato poked into the cage, and if the opossum ate the sweet potato, the person whose name had accompanied its offering became a suspect. Then the opossum was killed and a caterpillar named for each suspect was wrapped in a banana leaf and bound to its body. The opossum was roasted, the leaves opened and the caterpillars examined for any sign of life. If a living caterpillar bore a person's name, he was the sorcerer and must be killed. But if the opossum had been well cooked, no killer would be found. This held true in the investigation of Matante's death. The opossum was eaten, as were the caterpillars, and the case was considered closed.

21

*F*OR THE PLAIN SATISFACTION *of living, of being about their business in some sort or other, do the brave, serviceable men of every nation tread down the nettle danger, and pass flyingly over all the stumbling blocks of prudence.* Lesley closed the volume of Stevenson's essays on her thumb and mulled over the sentence, diagramming it in her mind. She looked up "nettle" in her *American Heritage* and discovered its tertiary definition to be "to sting with or as if with a nettle;" its secondary "to irritate; vex." Plain satisfaction, she thought. Plain satisfaction seemed to characterize Russell and to be all that Nick lacked. In Nick's case, it was everything. Everything vexed him because he had no capacity for enjoyment. But it hadn't always been so.

Until Katy came along, she had never felt quite so loved as she had during the ten months she and Nick shared between the day of their wedding and his being ordered to Viet Nam. As an officer in the Transportation Corps, he seemed to have acquired the sense of identity he had longed for. He was officially someone, and their life seemed to be unfolding before them like the predictable plot of a fifties movie.

At Fort Eustis, Virginia, Lesley attended orientation seminars for new Army wives and devoted the remainder of her time to preparing herself and their off-base apartment for Nick's nightly return from his advanced training classes. She experimented with recipes from the *I Hate To Cook Book*, studied manuals with titles like *How To Be A Happily Married Mistress*, and fantasized about their life together with the children they would have when he returned from Viet Nam.

As the time of Nick's tour of duty drew closer, their lovemaking took on a desperate quality, as if they hoped to glut their desire for each other as insulation against parting. Lesley let Nick take nude Polaroids of her, which he promised solemnly to let no one else see, and they exchanged tiny bouquets of pubic hair bound together with satin ribbons.

Russell found a small house for Lesley in Five Oaks, and he looked in on her frequently during Nick's absence. Lesley was charmed by Russell's attention and by his somewhat bashful courtliness. She imagined him as what Nick would be in middle age, and this both pleased her and intensified her longing.

During the early weeks of his tour, Nick's letters arrived almost daily, filled with expressions of love and carnal yearning. She read them over in the evenings and occasionally took them to her bedroom, where she satisfied herself as she imagined Nick might from his descriptions of what he would do if he were home.

But after two months, his letters tapered off and focused more and more on the horror and eventual numbness of unloading transport planes filled with replacements, who, he wrote, looked like children in soldier suits, and of reloading the yawning bays with the dispirited and frequently mutilated bodies of veterans going home. He wrote of a night helicopter flight to a supply base in the central highlands, of tracer rounds like tubes of neon light streaming into the jungle darkness and the door-gunner taking return fire through the throat, of the incomprehensible volume of blood, the warmth of it soaking into Nick's uniform as the gunner died in his arms.

By the end of his sixth month, when he had been transferred to Graves Registration, he no longer wrote of the war or of what he was doing, and his letters diminished to obligatory communiques.

Dear Lesley, More of the same here. Hope everything's okay there. I miss you. Love, Nick

It seemed to her now that, apart from his having made the effort to discover her name and to call her for their first date, Nick's having left her for Philippa was the most decisive action he had taken in the eighteen years she had known him. The difficulties of their marriage had been not those of a clash of wills but rather the lack of a will to clash with, no sounding board for her ideas or her aspirations. Nick always took the line of least resistance. His responses to her enthusiasms were predictably limited to indifference or sullen acquiescence, which, after incubation, inevitably erupted in a blizzard of invective, a begging for forgiveness and a desperate need to be reassured that she still loved him.

One month before the cease-fire and seventy-two hours after his last glimpse of the Vietnamese coast from the window of a chartered Northwest Orient 707, Nick was back in Five Oaks. He hadn't written to inform her of his arrival. He hadn't written at all in the previous six weeks. He gave a taxi driver one hundred dollars to drive him the seventy-five miles from the airport near Grand Rapids and rang the doorbell of their rented house while Lesley was making coffee on a Sunday morning in February.

The uniformed figure in the doorway looked very much like the man she had dreamed her life around, but this slightly thinner and considerably less animated version behaved more as if he had just returned from a trip to the newsstand for the funny papers. Her outburst of joy and surprise echoed back at her from his implacable face and made her feel foolish. He held his olive-green trench coat in one hand and his duffel in the other and dropped neither in order to return her embrace. Lesley attributed his lassitude to the fatigue of his flight and the shock of being so suddenly back home. But Nick's lethargy didn't wear off, and as the weeks went by she realized that it wasn't simply a temporary condition. She tried to pick up where they'd left off, as if trying to recreate the last scene in an interrupted play, but Nick wasn't playing anymore.

When she told him she had taken a job with the Wing County Department of Social Services, he merely shrugged and mumbled, "That's nice," as if she had just told him that a neighbor had dropped off a dozen ears of sweet corn. It wasn't until her work schedule came into conflict with his plans for them to spend a long weekend in Chicago that he expressed any interest in the matter, telling her she could take her job and shove it. Lesley traded cases with another worker in the department and spent most of the weekend on her own at the Art Institute and the Museum of Science and Industry while Nick holed up in their hotel room drinking beer and watching movies on television.

He took a job with Wheeler Industries because it was there for him. He joined the country club, began playing golf, and adopted television as his religion. Except for her expressed desire for a child, he accepted every suggestion Lesley made, and initiated nothing.

When he had been home several months, she tried to talk about it while they sat having a drink on the small screened porch off their kitchen. They'd just returned from seeing a movie on an unseasonably warm night for early May, and they could hear the Beatles singing "Eleanor Rigby" through the open window of the house across their backyard.

"You don't seem very happy," she said. "You don't seem to get enthused about anything."

"Oh?" Nick took a long swallow from his scotch and water. "What should I get enthused about?"

"I wasn't thinking of anything in particular. Life, baseball, me, your work. I don't know, music, the movies."

"You think I should get excited about the movies?" There was no discernable irritation in his voice.

"Not the movies necessarily, but as an example."

"An example of what?"

"I don't know, something to care about."

"You think I don't care?"

"I know you must. I know you. You just don't seem to let it show anymore."

"No, you're wrong. I don't care. And I don't want to."

"Oh come on Nick, that's not true."

"Don't tell me what's true."

"I know you saw a lot of things that were pretty horrible, but . . ."

"You don't know what I've seen," he interrupted.

"No, you're right; I don't, not exactly."

"Not at all, exactly!" he shouted.

"Nick, what are you blaming me for?"

He expelled a breath, sharply. It sounded to her as if he was laughing to himself in the darkness. "I'm not blaming anybody for anything. I just want you to mind your own goddamned business." His voice was controlled and emphatic.

"Oh?" Lesley sat and listened a moment. The Beatles were singing "Nowhere Man." "You're my husband. I thought you were my business."

"I'm going to bed," he muttered. He stood up and groped his way toward the kitchen door.

22

Now for the first time not on business, having no agenda or corporate identity, Russell saw concourse G at La Guardia as a gallery of lives, any one of which might have been his. In the men's room he watched a man about his own age pathetically trying to shave a five-day beard with a rusty Gillette razor he had probably found in a trash bin. Without any conscious intention, Russell found himself moving one sink further away from the man. He felt slightly ashamed that he had done this. It wasn't just the sour smell of the man, though there was that too, but a fear, he realized, that the man might try to speak to him. Did he ever have a family, Russell wondered, a job?

What did he do, and when did he stop doing it?

In the baggage claim area he saw another man, a vice-president of Weyerhauser with whom he had served on the board of the American Pulp Association. A prickly heat spread over his face and through his scalp. His heart raced, and he turned away so that he wouldn't be recognized. Russell had no reason to avoid this man—Arthur Wyatt was his name. He remembered liking him. Keeping his back to Arthur Wyatt, he walked to a pay phone just beyond the turnstile and called the Carlyle Hotel where he normally stayed, and where anyone who should happen to spot him would assume he could be reached. He cancelled his reservation and looked in the Yellow Pages for another hotel in the same part of the city. He was able to book a room at the Stanhope for immediate arrival, and when he returned to pick up his bag, Arthur Wyatt was gone.

He took a taxi to the Stanhope, checked in and called

Marlis' apartment. There was no answer. He looked at his watch; it was 4:45. She was probably still at her office. He could call her there, he thought. But no, he would wait. He wondered if she really was happy living in New York, but the question seemed silly. She'd been there twenty years. She had her own public relations firm, a small one made up of herself and two associates, which did work for small companies under contract. She had money from the Wheeler stock he had given her and didn't need the income, but he could understand her satisfaction in making something work and grow. But is that enough, he wondered. She seemed content though she had never married; at forty-five, she probably never would.

He took the elevator down to the lobby, left the hotel and crossed the street. He walked the length of the Metropolitan Museum having no destination, no purpose in mind. He felt conspicuous, as he did sometimes walking into a store with no clear intention of making a purchase, and so he set a course for himself. He would walk down Fifth Avenue to 49th Street and then back up Madison, which would kill enough time for Marlis to finish her work and get back to her apartment.

It was a mild November afternoon, sunny and with only a trifling breeze, pleasant for walking. The trees in the park, sere and rustling in the acute amber light, still held more of their last leaves than did the trees back home. He was no one, walking in a city unconscious of its beauty, as if he had caught it off guard. Or had it caught him?

Below 58th Street, the aspect changed. Great monoliths walled in the avenue and blocked out the light. They denied any possibility of life behind their obsidian facades; jealousies, triumphs, affronts and affectations were all masked by their passionless grandeur.

On Madison it seemed to him that most of the people were in costume. They mirrored his conception of the Upper East Side like caricatures in a movie: an elderly European couple, their faces projecting a practiced ennui, enjoyed their ritual stroll past the galleries (she in a fox stole and ebony cane, he in a vicuna coat and a homburg); two death-pale girls in black tights with clown eye shadow and bright blue hair. What could they be thinking, he wondered. Could they be thinking? He stopped to watch a model in a street-length white mink being photographed in front of a church. She was stunning, of course, but no more so than any number of women he had passed. No matter how often he came to New York he never became accustomed to the plethora of exotic-looking women. Did New Yorkers surfeit themselves with such beauty or did they only feign indifference? Lesley would turn heads, even here, he thought. He wished she could be there with him now. Were there any ordinary people in New York? Would he be ordinary in the eyes of these people, or did they even consider such things? Russell smiled at his speculations, and then laughed quietly as it occured to him that smiling out of context in New York would definitely make him conspicuous.

He was thinking of Lesley when he stopped to look in the window of a store that dealt in ancient Greek and Roman artifacts. There was a gold necklace set with a silver coin bearing the likeness of a woman in a Grecian helmet. The woman on the coin reminded him of Lesley, and he went into the store and bought it for her. What would she think of his giving it to her? What would other people think? And did it matter? The right woman at the right time, he thought. And suddenly he remembered something and was overcome with embarrassment. When Nick was in the 9th grade he had come into Russell's den. After some nervous talk about school, Nick told him that he wanted to get some experience with women and asked Russell if he didn't think it might be a good idea if he went to visit a prostitute. Russell prided himself on the idea of always having been quite frank with his children, but Nick's question shocked him. He told Nick that sex could either be the most beautiful experience he could have or else something pretty ugly. "It all depends on if it's right or not," he said. "The right woman at the right time." There followed an uncom-

fortable silence which he had finally broken by suggesting
that Nick take a drive with him up north of Bitely to look
over the new timberlands the company had acquired.

"I think some of the guys are coming over," Nick said.

Russell blushed as he thought back on it and wondered if
there wasn't some limit on the time beyond which past ac-
tions would no longer return to embarrass him. He lingered
in front of a market, admiring the sausages which hung like
boughs of holly along the borders of the window, shading
filets, Delmonicos, liver, lamb chops, and pork loins. He
realized he was hungry and began to relish the idea of a
good dinner with Marlis.

It was 6:30 when he called her apartment again. The
phone rang three times and then a man answered.

"I'm sorry," Russell said. "I think I've dialed the wrong
number."

"Who are you calling?" the man asked.

"I was calling 294-5777."

"This is it!" There was an unnatural enthusiasm in the
man's voice.

"Is this Marlis Wheeler's phone?"

"None other," the man said. "Would you like to speak
with her?"

"Please." Russell's mind flipped through possibilities like
a rolodex. Had Marlis told him about a man, and had he
forgotten?

"Hello."

"Marlis, hello."

"Who is this?"

"It's your father, of course." How could she not know,
he thought.

"Dad! Where are you?"

"At the Stanhope, room 929."

"You mean you're in New York? What are you doing
here? I thought you'd retired."

"That doesn't mean I can't come to New York, does it?"

"No, of course not. But I mean what are you doing?
Does it have to do with Nick?"

"Well, yes." Obviously she'd heard from Nick, he thought. "But I came to see you."

"That's wonderful. I just wish you'd give me some warning."

"Warning? I didn't come to kill you."

"I didn't mean warning. You know that. It's just such a surprise. You're usually more predictable."

"Maybe I'm changing. I'm becoming impulsive."

"My father, impulsive?"

"I wasn't always your father, you know."

"You were to me."

"I guess that's right." Russell laughed. "Are you free for dinner?"

"I can get free for you."

"Would your friend like to join us?"

"My friend?" She sounded slightly alarmed.

"The man who answered the phone."

"Oh no, I don't think so. Raoul has plans. You make a reservation at someplace terribly expensive, and I'll be at your hotel at eight."

AS THEY FOLLOWED THE MAITRE D' to their banquette at La Reserve, Russell noticed that Marlis was heavier than he remembered. It had been almost two years. Was that possible? He had dined with her when he was in town to address the Newcoman Society. That had been at least a year before he had retired. How could so much time have gone by?

They began with a bottle of Montrachet, and the clear sharp taste of it put Russell in a festive mood. He was having an adventure and, though his intention was principally to learn what he could about Nick, at the moment he felt no urgency about his mission. He was hungry, the wine was teasing his appetite, he was being a responsible father and enjoying the company of his daughter. Russell ordered *escargot en croute* and Marlis a terrine of duck liver. They finished the Montrachet, ordered a rare '49 Latour with their rack of lamb, and talked about Marlis' business. She had taken on several food companies and was touting them to the financial community. "The big thing today, as you know, is keeping the price of the stock up as a defense against takeovers. It's something no one thought about ten years ago that everyone thinks about now. It seems to me that business is becoming all manipulation. No wonder the Japanese are on a roll. They still care about producing goods and services."

"Have you heard from Nick?" Russell asked, wondering in hindsight how abrupt this shift seemed.

"Yes, I have. You know I have."

For the first time, Russell saw Marlis as one of those wise spinsters who were the backbone of so many organizations.

"He feels as if he's busted out," Marlis continued.

"Busted out?"

"He's confused, of course, and feels badly about letting everyone down. He actually cried about it when we first talked. But he's also excited about being here, about the possibilities."

"I guess I can understand that," Russell said. "He's been trying to be a good boy all his life."

"I'm surprised to hear you say that."

"I know. I'm probably the main reason for it. He wanted to please me. And I was pleased. I was pleased with his choice of a wife, pleased he chose to go into the business. The only thing he forgot to do was to please himself."

"I'm happy you can see that," Marlis said. "I sort of expected you to be on the war path about what you would normally call irresponsible behavior."

"Oh, I was at first, but you'd be surprised. I was angry over the hurt he caused Lesley. But age can wake you up to a lot of things."

"You're hardly what I'd call geriatric." Marlis smiled. "In fact you're still really quite an attractive man."

"Thank you, that's nice to hear. But what I mean is that I'm old enough to know that I really am going to die, and that changes the way you look at a lot of things. Some of the things I once thought were all-important just don't seem as interesting to me anymore, things like money and

success and responsibility." He spoke the last word with ex-
aggerated enunciation.

"You don't disappoint me." Marlis raised her glass to
him.

"Thank you." Russell raised his glass. "And you." He
drank to her. "You've surprised me all along. I'd have
thought you'd have been married three or four times by
now."

"I'd have thought so too, twenty-five years ago."

"Do you ever think about marriage anymore?"

"No. Never."

"What about Raoul?"

"Oh, Raoul," Marlis laughed. "Raoul's just a good
friend. He's not the marrying kind."

"Do you mean he's gay?"

"Yes, I do mean that."

"Is there any man in the picture right now?"

"No, not in the way you mean. Did you want there to
be?"

"No. It's your life. I just worry sometimes. I don't want
you to be lonely."

"Aren't you lonely?"

"Yes, sometimes I am."

"Well, I'm not lonely," Marlis said. "And I want to tell
you something I've wanted you to know for a long time. I
don't live alone. I have a friend, a lover."

"But you said . . ." Russell was genuinely confused.

"I said there was no man."

"You mean . . . ?" For an instant Russell felt as if his chair
was sinking into the floor.

"Yes. I mean that my lover is a woman. I've been with
her almost two years now. It isn't that I don't like men. I
just don't like them in that way anymore, the way I like
Elizabeth."

Russell swallowed down his windpipe and broke into a
fit of coughing. One of the captains made his way toward
their table in alarm, but Russell displayed his palm to indicate that he was okay, and the captain bowed courteously

and retreated. "I'm sorry," Russell said hoarsely, when he began to regain control of his voice. "I mean this is kind of a surprise."

"Don't you mean a shock?" Marlis asked wryly.

"Well, yes it is." Russell cleared his throat. "I mean how did this happen?" His face was flushed and his eyes had the same sad dazed look Marlis had seen when he had told her that her mother was leaving him.

"How did what happen?" There was a defensive, determined tone about her question.

"Everything." Russell coughed again. "Everyone leaving me. Did I drive everyone away?"

"Don't be silly." Marlis laughed cynically. "It doesn't have anything to do with you. I haven't left you, anymore than I did when I moved to New York twenty years ago. It's my life we're talking about, not yours. How would you have felt if I'd told you I had a male lover or that I'd decided to get married?"

"I'm sorry," Russell said. He paused to take a deep breath. "I just always pictured . . ." He paused again, waiting for the appropriate word to come to him. "Ah, gay women . . ."

"Lesbians?" Marlis suggested.

"Yes." Russell nodded. "I always thought of them as hard, bitter women."

"Some are. But so are a lot of heterosexual women."

"Well, that's right," Russell agreed. "I'm not upset. I'm really not. It's just something I never considered."

"I know." Marlis smiled and put her hand on his shoulder. "You've had a lot of surprises. But I want you to know about me. I've always looked up to you, I've loved you, and I want you to know who I am."

"Well . . . I love you too. And I'm happy for you, if you're happy. I mean that." Russell smiled and shook his head. "But I don't understand why. You always had lots of dates. You were boy crazy."

"That's not a question I can answer. Why was I born a

woman? Why were you born male? I had a miscarriage when I was in college—"

"But . . ." Russell started to speak, but Marlis put her hand over his to quiet him.

"I know, I never told you I was pregnant. I couldn't bring myself to do it. I knew how you felt about that, how disappointed you'd have been. But I wanted the child. I wanted to marry the man."

While Marlis was talking Russell listened, but he couldn't help noticing a color etching of hooded mergansers on the wall behind her head and remembering the last dinner he'd had here, with Miriam, after they'd agreed to divorce yet remain good friends, the strained quality of their conversation as they tiptoed around any subject that might open old wounds or recriminations. Had he been blind all those years, he wondered, or just not paying attention? He remembered the silences that had sometimes gone on for days, each of them waiting for the other to broach the subject of Miriam's drinking or his neglect, of his infidelities which Miriam couldn't forgive or of Miriam's which he chose to ignore.

"I thought I loved him." Marlis squeezed his hand as she spoke. "And I was horrified by what was happening to me, by the thought that I was letting our baby die there in that dormitory bathroom with blood all over the tile, and I didn't want anything like that to ever happen again. Maybe that was part of it. I do like men, or boys. That one was a boy. He sent me some flowers, and I never saw him again. Maybe it is your fault. Maybe I just never found any man I thought measured up to you."

"You must have a pretty unreal notion of who I am."

"Probably. But I'm not unhappy about it. I'm forty-five years old. I like men. I love you. I just don't want to get involved with them, that's all. I love Elizabeth. I want to spend the rest of my life with her. I got spoiled as far as men were concerned. Why don't you just take it as a compliment?"

"I do. I just think I went astray somewhere, giving you a distorted picture."

"Oh, I expect you've got your dark side. I expect that if you weren't my father and we tried to be lovers, I'd find something about you I didn't like, some reason it wouldn't work out."

"Your mother found those chinks in my armor. And I found them in hers. That's just being human."

"And you're not together anymore."

"No. But some people are. Some people make it work."

"Elizabeth and I are still together. We're making it work. It's just the fact that we're both women which offends your sensibilities."

"Well no, not really. I don't feel that way." Russell blushed. "It confounds my expectations, that's all. But I'm not offended. I want you to be happy. And if this is the way you're happy . . ."

"Most men aren't that understanding, most straight men."

"How do you know I'm straight?"

"Oh I know." Marlis had tears in her eyes. "You're as straight as they come, and I love you for it."

AFTER DINNER HE TOOK MARLIS to the Cafe Carlyle where they listened to the piano music of Marian McPartland. Marlis told him that she thought it would be best if he didn't try to contact Nick just yet.

"But I want him to know that I love him," Russell said.

"I'll tell him that." Marlis patted his hand. "And I know it'll mean a lot to him now, knowing it doesn't depend on his pleasing you."

"I'd like to think it never did."

"Maybe so, but Nick didn't know that."

"Okay. But please tell him that. Maybe we could get to be friends."

"Maybe, Dad. Maybe it'll just take time."

They listened to a medley of Cole Porter tunes. Russell was thinking about Lesley and wondering how Marlis, for all her matter-of-factness about her own life, would react if she knew the kinds of thoughts he was entertaining about Lesley, the kinds of thoughts he was telling himself he must not entertain.

The medly ended with "It's All Right With Me," and as they finished applauding, Marlis turned to Russell and said, "Since this is a night for confessions, I want to know something about you. Did you ever have an affair?"

Russell looked at the pink tablecloth before him and then at the brandy snifter in his hand. "Yes," he nodded. "Yes I did, more than once." He lit Marlis's cigarette. "It seems odd, confessing this to you. It's odd because I don't feel any guilt about it."

"Should you?"

"Abstractly I think I should. But then I don't live in an abstract world. Right now I don't feel guilty at all. But at the time, when I came back to face your mother, I felt tremendous guilt."

"You must've known she was seeing other men."

"I sensed it, but I wouldn't let myself think it, if that makes any sense." He wanted to tell her how he felt about Lesley, to see if he was completely crazy or monstrous to even be thinking about it, but he couldn't bring himself to do it.

"You mean you didn't want to believe it." Marlis tapped the ash off her cigarette. For a moment it seemed to Russell that she'd taken on the persona of a prosecutor.

"Yes."

"What would you have done if I'd told you she was?"

"At the time you mean?"

"Yes."

"I'd have hated you, I'm sure."

"I think I knew that. I wanted to tell you. I wanted to tell someone. I always used to think you were blind, but now I realize you were just trying to hold things together. I hated the idea that she thought she was getting away with it."

"She was, and she wasn't. She was bored. And that was my fault. I chose to be numb to anything or anyone I didn't understand. I was numb to you and Nick. Most of my life hasn't seemed quite real to me."

"I think you're ahead of the game. Most people are that way, but they just don't know it. I forgot who it was who said that if you're aware of your delusion you're not really deluded."

"I must've been willfully deluded. But I'm proud of you and Nick whatever you do."

"That's nice to hear."

"Even at forty-five?"

"Especially at forty-five."

"I'm only sorry it took so long to say it."

Before he put her in a cab on Madison, Russell accepted Marlis' invitation to dine with her and Elizabeth the following evening. And as he walked back to his hotel, he thought how life seemed to take a perverse pleasure in confounding his expectations. Was that it, complacency, he wondered. Had he been asleep to the life around him? He didn't think so. It was just bigger and more diverse than he could ever imagine. And thinking that, he felt an unaccountable lightness, as if there were no substantial difference between his life and the mist he now felt coating his face.

23

I~T WAS ODD, THE IDEA~ of a day in New York with no
agenda. When he woke he thought about stopping by the
New York office or calling David Gould at the agency for
lunch. But no, he would spend the day alone. Why should
that seem like a challenge? He smiled, remembering a pas-
sage from a book of legends Lesley had recommended, in
which Arthur's knights, setting forth in search of the Grail,
declared that "they thought it would be a disgrace to enter
the forest in a group." He would be a solitary knight.
Though, like Parzival dreaming of Condwiramurs, he
couldn't help thinking how nice it would be if Lesley were
there to show him the Met.

When he returned to his hotel just after 5:00, he was tired
but glad for his weariness; it helped ease his anxiety about
meeting Elizabeth. He was nervous about saying something that might inadvertantly offend. He had never spent
any time around lesbians. The word had an oddly geo-
graphical ring to it, like Latvians. A lesbian marriage.

He fixed himself a bourbon and water from the mini-bar
and toyed with the sound of it. They were American girls,
after all. Girls, women. Marlis. I can't fault them, he
thought. If I were a woman I might be a lesbian.

At the Metropolitan Museum he had wandered by
chance into the Michael Rockefeller Wing and found himself facing a reconstructed spirit house from New Guinea.
For a moment he heard the moaning of flutes and smelled
the sweet rancid odor of the People, an odor unmatched in
forty years. When he came to a display of ceremonial
masks, he saw Kopa ki's face as he had last seen it, falling

away from him into the jungle. "Take me with you, Quari," a voice said. It spoke through shining brown eyes and an eager smile, half-obscured by ritual scarring and a scimitar-like piece of bone worn through the nose like an inverted mustache. Then the face dissolved into a fierce carved smile and tufts of pig bristle. He walked on to the Temple of Dendur and spent the rest of the morning contemplating life in ancient Egypt.

After lunch in the museum cafeteria he set off to walk thirty blocks down the avenue to Saks, but after only five blocks he felt unaccountably fatigued and hailed a cab. He wandered the floors of Saks, looking for nothing in particular, least of all the fantasies engendered by the perfume of the women he passed in first floor cosmetics. He imagined the lives of women he followed on the escalator. He decided to buy something for Lesley, forgetting the pendant he had purchased the day before. Shopping was a way of loving without having to commit, enjoying an affair he could never consummate, free of the risk of rejection or disgrace. He settled on a pink-flowered white flannel nightgown, suggestive yet appropriately chaste. He told the saleswoman it was for his wife.

On his way back uptown he stopped at F.A.O. Schwartz, bought a huge stuffed tiger as a Christmas present for Katy and arranged to have it shipped.

At the Stanhope, he fixed himself another bourbon and water and called Lesley to tell her what he had, or hadn't, learned about Nick.

"But I'll try to reach him if Marlis will give me the number."

"Russell, I hope you're not doing this for me. I accepted the fact of his being gone a long time ago."

"I miss you," he said before hanging up. He wondered if his words had sounded suitably paternal, or if he had meant them to be.

RUSSELL'S APPREHENSIONS about dinner with Marlis and Elizabeth were quickly dispelled by their candor and their easy, unobtrusive way with each other. Like sisters, Russell thought, or good friends who have sex. Their apartment seemed quite conventional. It was decorated in pastel blues with Audubon birds and floral prints, rather than the feminist posters and black lights he had half-imagined. He sat in a wing chair enjoying both his drink and the smell of the cassoulet Elizabeth was tending while Marlis prepared a salad with artichokes and avocados. Elizabeth was pretty in a slightly chubby Snow White sort of way, quite feminine, not at all the way he had imagined a lesbian, but then neither was Marlis. He couldn't help feeling a little jealousy over the idea that two such attractive women had removed themselves from the arena, that whatever the circumstances Elizabeth would have no interest in him. Marlis's friend. Marlis's girlfriend, ladyfriend. How would he refer to her, he wondered, if the situation arose?

They had met at a neighborhood Gristede's several years ago, Elizabeth explained. They had both been shopping for rice to make risotto and had gotten into a discussion over which rice was best suited and whether or not it was necessary to stir in the broth over a full twenty minutes, as Elizabeth contended, or if it could be added all at once, the time-saving method favored by Marlis. They had agreed to invite each other to their respective apartments for risotto dinners to test their ideas and Marlis had eventually conceded that Elizabeth's more demanding technique was worth the extra effort, though she doubted she would bother with it on her own. "In fact, I concluded that Elizabeth was a far better cook all around," Marlis said. "And that may well be because she enjoys it more than I do. You might even accuse me of marrying her for her cooking." She winked at Russell.

"Marrying?" Russell was having his third glass of Vouvray.

"Figure of speech," Elizabeth said, reaching out and squeezing his hand, as Marlis had the previous evening.

"Would that make you figuratively my daughter-in-law?"

"Figuratively, I guess it would," Elizabeth smiled. "Though already I like you better than my former father-in-law, Russ."

"You were married?"

"Yes. We were married when I was seventeen. His name was Roger, and he never appreciated my cooking."

"Well, good riddance to Roger, then." Russell raised his glass.

"The toast is good riddance to Roger," Elizabeth chimed in, clinking glasses with Marlis and Russell.

"And what about Nick, then?" Russell interjected. "Is he happy with this new woman, Philippa?"

"She's not really new," Marlis responded. "He's been seeing her for several years. He feels he's really somebody with her; that's how he puts it. I think she's someone who doesn't intimidate him."

"Did Lesley intimidate him?"

"I think we all did, to some degree. If you step back and look at us we're a pretty intimidating bunch. I think Nick's always felt a little out of his league, as if the stork dropped him down the wrong chimney. That's the way he perceived it, anyway. He didn't care about anything until Philippa came along."

"You don't think I should talk to him?"

"I think he needs a little more time."

They were silent for a moment. Marlis looked at Russell quizzically, as if questioning whether he really understood.

"Pardon my curiosity," Russell turned to Elizabeth and paused to consider his question. "If you don't mind talking about it, were there other men in your life besides Roger?"

"No, I don't mind talking about it. Yes, there were other men. Quite a few lovers, but not many friends. I wanted both, wanted to be both. But the men who were interested in me sexually always ended up treating me more like a member of an inferior species than simply as a different gender. I just never found the tenderness I needed, the companionship, until I met Marlis."

Russell noticed his daughter blush. "So it's really a very close friendship?"

"Shouldn't any marriage be?" Elizabeth asked. "Shouldn't it grow out of that?"

"Well, yes. I guess it should," Russell said, mulling it over. "Marlis and I are friends who enjoy doing what we can to please each other."

"God, I wish my marriage had been like that," Russell laughed. "Excuse me Marlis, but you understand."

Marlis nodded. "I understand very well."

"So you think any kind of a relationship is okay as long as the people care for each other?" He looked at Marlis as he asked the question.

"Yes, I do. Any two people who care enough to take good care of each other."

Russell smiled broadly as Marlis spoke. The wine had done its work and relieved him of his usual inhibition against fantasizing in the presence of others, an inhibition fostered by a nagging suspicion that they might possibly be able to read his thoughts. He wasn't sure he had ever really considered Marlis in a sexual way. At least he had never imagined having sex with her, and he had never wanted to imagine her carnally engaged with any of the boys she had dated. But there in the room with them and bouyed by the untrammeled discussion they were having, he pictured she and Elizabeth tenderly exploring each other to the point that he felt himself becoming aroused. And he imagined Lesley there in a dreamlike montage of lips, breasts, thighs and tangled hair.

Elizabeth poured more wine, and Russell toasted, "To love and friendship."

They drank to it.

WELL, RUSSELL THOUGHT to himself on the cab ride back to his hotel, however I failed my children, Marlis is happy at least, at last, and I won't let Lesley or Katy be unhappy if I can do anything about it. Or me either. The cab jolted over some potholes on Third Avenue and as Russell rearranged himself on the seat he thought with some satisfaction that Marlis would approve, in principle at least.

24

Even in the mirror of his hotel bathroom, tinted to flatter, the face that looked back at him as he brushed his teeth looked old. Old as he had thought of old as a child, a childhood that didn't seem very long ago. He reflected how all the events of one's life between a particular memory and the present fall into oblivion so that any experience brought vividly to mind seems only yesterday. He rinsed his mouth and examined the darkness around his eyes. It was his eyes that looked old. Maybe it was all the wine. He still had a full head of hair, gray hair he had once thought of as distinguished salt and pepper. It seemed to have hidden the years so that he might pass for . . . oh, fifty-five, maybe. What does fifty-five look like, he wondered? But those eyes. Wouldn't anything he saw through eyes like those look old? *You are not what it is, but it is what you are.* A phrase from one of the Japanese or Chinese books Lesley had given him, something he had puzzled over. "You are not me, but I am you." He spoke to the confused face in the mirror. "Or no, the other way around." The fool. Was he playing the fool, trying to become young again for his fantasy lover? He wondered if all he had denied himself might have been simply a result of cowardice, if he hadn't hidden behind propriety from some larger vision of himself he had been afraid to confront. He remembered Boy Wheeler in one of his eyes-on-the-horizon moods once saying that a man of spirit knew no boundaries. And he wondered how much more Boy might have made out of the circumstances of his life if they had been able to exchange situations. Boy would probably have left Miriam long before she left him. He would have loved Nick more or at least expressed his love more freely. He would have given him more attention. The other Russell would have enjoyed his life in Five Oaks every day, as he had remembered to do only on occasion. Where do you lose your youth, he wondered. In the numbness of days? The absence of love? Or had he lost it way back in New Guinea? And was he trying now to siphon it from Lesley? He stepped back and the reflection in the mirror seemed to shift. Old fool, he thought fondly. But nothing was ever really done without risking the fool. Would he risk what he had now by trying to make more of it? Hadn't he always done that? Nick. So much unhappiness she's had with Nick. Nick of my making. Could I make her happy? Or would I just compound it? Like son, like father, like son. Lesley, my daughter, but not like Marlis. More than my daughter. What's the decent thing? The decent thing. Always the decent thing. The eternal misery of the decent thing. A decent life, a decent death. My mother who made a career of decency, weak-chinned, milk-faced decency. Decency or joy, one is forced to choose. Decent, decent, de-scent. Going down? Pass it on. Decent money, a decent wage. I'm drunk. So what? *In vino veritas.* I think I haven't been drunk enough.

He steadied himself against the doorjamb, then worked his way from the desk to the dresser to the bed and collapsed. Lesley, Lesley, Lesley. Don't be afraid. Let me tell you something. Then you forget it, okay? I'm not a dirty old man. Old maybe, but not dirty. Well maybe a little. Okay, I'm a dirty old man. *Tis certain lovely women eat a crazy salad with their meat.* Some people even like succotash. Ugh! Don't think about succotash. Or brussels sprouts. Ugh! Don't think. Don't think.

25

Down below a metal roof or a solar panel caught a ray of sunlight and reflected it back up to him at thirty-five thousand feet. How often he had seen that vast miniature world from the window of a plane and mused about how lonely it would be to live down there in western Pennsylvania or eastern Ohio simply because it wasn't home to him, how invisible he would be in that expanse, his troubles and triumphs reduced to scale in a new landscape. He thought also of how often he had made this trip thinking of Miriam, his heart and his libido keyed with an absence of a week or even a few days, imagining a homecoming that seldom panned out. He would indulge himself, remembering the best times or fragments of times when they had shared a kind of bliss or what he chose to remember as bliss. But he would arrive home to rediscover that his priorities were not Miriam's and that the lust he fostered was his alone.

Eventually they would make love, but without the ardor he imagined they had once shared and only after she had accomplished a maddening variety of household tasks she apparently hadn't had time for while he was away. Sometimes Miriam's friend, Mildred Wallace, would be there when the company driver brought him home from the airport, and Miriam would be sipping wine, listening with apparently rapt attention to some banal account of a trip to Chicago or a party at the country club in which she would normally have had no interest. On and on they talked, on this of all nights, until Russell would take his dog, who had been genuinely glad to see him, and walk out under the stars remembering that he had turned down the woman at the Trade Center reception because he hadn't wanted to compromise what he had chosen to remember as his happy marriage.

Had it been that way for Nick with Lesley? Or had it been the other way around? He wanted to believe that Lesley had been scorned in every effort she had made to please Nick. It was never just one way, though sometimes it seemed so. He thought of Janice Poole, the creative director with Weston & Gould, a ballet dancer who would squat over him on the balls of her feet anytime he was in town, her hands on his ribs for balance, and describe every sensation she felt as she was feeling it. Or Patricia Clark, the girl he had met on a flight to Seattle who thought she was in love with him until he had convinced her he would never leave Miriam and the children. There were times when he felt justified because of Miriam's indifference, and other times when he came home wondering if the look on his face would betray what he had done and was feeling. And frequently it did. Miriam would talk a confession out of him and then shelve it for future use, saying, "I know you'll do whatever you please," or, "If that's what you need for your ego."

There had also been Jane Gifford, Marlis's high school friend, who escorted him around campus when he accepted an invitation to give a lecture on reforestation at her college. She invited him back to her apartment after the faculty dinner in his honor and spoke wistfully about the thoughtlessness of her high school lovers and of how few college men seemed to "really understand a young woman's needs." Among Marlis's friends, Russell had always paid particular attention to Jane, noting the directness of her gaze, her slightly bucked teeth, her awareness of the way her bottom complemented a pair of jeans and the effect she knew it had on him. In her apartment that evening they sipped cheap wine and her frankness elicited his agreement about, among other things, the callowness of young men and the maturity of so many young women. She sat facing him on her couch, legs curled up under her so that her skirt rode up over her knees and he could see the pure whiteness of her panties. The heat of her thighs was palpable. He wanted her desperately but made excuses about the hour and left her with a kiss on the cheek and a hug made a little more than filial by the pressure of her pelvis. On his drive home, late that night, he pulled onto the shoulder of the freeway and wept.

26

O NE SUMMER ON A TWO-WEEK DRIVE with Miriam in
their 1952 Buick convertible, Russell turned off on a ridge
of Big Lue Mountain overlooking the valley of the Gila
River in southeastern Arizona, and it seemed to him that
the entire earth lay below them, range after range of blue
mountains graying into the horizon. Russell was wearing a
sports jacket he had bought in a western store in Silver City,
New Mexico, a light beige coat with suede yokes which
Miriam thought gave him the look of a singing cowboy.
They laughed about the outfit, which was oddly striking
but at the same time ridiculous for a midwestern businessman. And Russell noted that this grandeur had been there
every day of their lives and that they had wasted thousands
of such days not seeing it. Miriam laughed about that too,
with some slight derision, he thought, but he let it pass.
Such moments were too rare to risk spoiling with analysis.
As he thought back on it now, he felt glad for what moments of closeness there had been, and as the plane made its
final approach to Grand Rapids, swaying and bucking in
the turbulence, he thought simply of how good it was to be
alive.

Lesley was waiting for him at the gate with Katy, and her
embrace was more enthusiastic than those he had recieved
from Miriam on such occasions. Yet he wondered if he
might be coloring it to suit his wishes, creating desires for
her she didn't share. "I missed you," he said.

"And I missed you," she whispered as she hugged him
again.

"I missed you too, Gamp," Katy laughed as he bent to

pick her up. She hugged him so tightly around the neck he thought his temples might burst.

As Lesley drove, he talked about Marlis, though not Elizabeth, about having heard Marian McPartland and about the Temple of Dendur at the Metropolitan Museum.

"Did you see my daddy?" Katy asked.

"No," Russell replied, unable to think of anything to add. He nuzzled her behind the ear and growled like a bear.

"You're silly," Katy giggled.

Russell glanced over at Lesley as she angled off onto the freeway ramp. "I picked up some fried rice and egg foo yung at the Great Eastern," she said.

"Perfect," Russell said. "It'll be a nice relief from all the French food I had in New York."

"Don't expect any sympathy from me," she laughed.

Russell admired the confidence with which Lesley maneuvered through the evening traffic.

BEFORE TAKING RUSSELL HOME, Lesley stopped at her house and dropped Katy off with a sitter. As it was still early evening, this seemed curious to Russell, but he refused to let himself speculate about any significance it might have.

Lily went mad with excitement over his return, yipping and scolding him for his absence and pawing his shin, hoping to elicit a Milkbone. He made her speak for it softly, then loudly, made her bow and then made her sit expectantly for a few seconds before he gave her permission to pick it up.

Lesley warmed up the Chinese food and uncorked a bottle of Piesporter while Russell unpacked. He removed the bag containing the white and pink flannel nightgown and laid it on the bed. He placed the small box containing the Greek pendant on top of it and wondered if he should give them to her tonight. He carried his toilet kit into the bathroom, then walked back to the door of the bedroom and hollered, "Do I have time for a shower?"

"Sure. This'll keep," Lesley called back to him.

As he lathered his hair, he forced down every thought

that tried to rise in his mind. The little he could tell Lesley of Nick, the great deal he now knew about Marlis, the fantasies he had entertained, the fears juggled and dismissed, the questions of propriety and desire, the nightgown, the face of Kopa ki in the spirit mask were all like sparks from a Roman wheel, spinning off as the water beat down on him like brilliant light. He took a deep breath, rubbed his hand over his eyes and reached for the towel.

It was a soft evening, perhaps the last of Indian summer. Lesley had opened the sliding glass doors to the porch, and as they picked at their dinner with rough wooden chopsticks they heard the quavering whistle of a screech owl from the forest and the reply of another, more distant. Russell refilled Lesley's wine glass.

"You'd almost think there should be crickets on a night like this," Lesley mused. "I find myself half-listening for them."

"I thought I'd heard them," Russell said. They were quiet for a moment, listening. "But I don't hear them now." He paused again, his ear cocked toward the door. "Thoreau says it's a sign of good health when a man can hear crickets."

"Assuming, of course, they're actually there to be heard." Lesley smiled.

"Yes, of course." Russell nodded. "But I carry my own crickets for nights like this." He could feel his heart pounding. "I wasn't able to contact Nick," he said.

Lesley reached out for his hand. "I hadn't expected you would. I know it must've been painful."

"I was thinking of you," Russell took her hand in both of his, "thinking what you must be going through."

"I went through it a long time ago. Now I'm more relieved than I am sad. I'm sad for Nick, of course. I hope he's found what he needs."

"I'm sorry, Lesley." Russell stroked her hands. "I'm sorry this all happened."

"Oh, I'm not. I'm not sorry. I have Katy, and I have you. You're the finest person I've ever known."

"You're seeing me the way you want to. The good gray father. But I'm not that. I never was."

"I know." She squeezed his hands.

"I got something for you in New York," he said.

"Russell . . ." Lesley started to speak, but he held up his hand to stop her. He got up, went to the bedroom, and returned with two packages.

"This one first." He handed her the blue velvet box, and she opened it.

"Oh Russell, it's beautiful." She held the necklace in her hand, and he could see her eyes just beginning to tear.

"It's Athena. She reminded me of you. I was being romantic, of course."

Lesley fastened it around her neck and parted the collar of her white blouse. "You are a fool," she smiled, "if you think of me as heroic."

"I do think of you that way." He layed his hand on her cheek.

"I love it." She leaned across the table and kissed him.

"There's something else." He reached down for the bag from Saks and set it on the table.

Lesley stood up, lifted the nightgown out of the bag and held it to her breast. "Oh Russell, it's sweet." She hugged him with the nightie pressed between them. "Is this how you think of me? All white and pink flowers?" She kissed him on the lips, lightly at first, and then more deeply. He felt his arms stiffen, felt the muscles in his shoulders and his neck contract as he held her away from him.

"What's wrong?" She looked at him with a curious, slightly hurt expression, her arms still around his neck.

"I don't know. I'm feeling shy. I guess I'm wondering if this is all right."

"All right according to whom?"

"I don't know. Some judge who was just here." He smiled. He inhaled some of her perfume and his smile faded.

"Is he gone now, the judge I mean?"

Russell nodded. He took her head in his hands and kissed her eyes and her forehead.

Lesley stepped back and looked up at him as if she were about to say something. Then she reached up and took him by the hand. "Come with me," she whispered. She led him through the hall and up the stairs to his bedroom. She lay down and pulled his hand until he was sitting beside her on the edge of the bed. "I want you," she whispered. "I've wanted this for a long time. Let's not spoil it with talk."

He stroked her shoulders and her neck, stroked the plain of her blouse above her breasts. He felt her tense and he froze, afraid for a moment as her head rose from the pillow and her tongue found his ear. "Russell, I'm a woman," she whispered, "I won't break." She slid around him, got up, and standing in front of him unbuttoned her blouse. She slipped out of her jeans, and then her panties. She unhooked her bra. She urged him to his feet and helped him out of his clothes. Then she lay back down on the bed and held her arms up to him. "Please," she whispered.

Russell knelt on the edge of the bed, stunned by her loveliness, the actuality of her nakedness, of her breathing, the rise and fall of her breasts, the dark tangle of pubic hair against the whiteness of her hips.

Lesley, my daughter, the thought came, and he pushed it away. "Lesley. This is hard for me to believe." He bent and kissed her on the knee. He felt her shiver.

"I know."

"I didn't plan this," he said.

She reached up to him, cupping his head in her hands, and drew his face to her breast. She kissed the top of his head as he explored the darkness of each nipple with his lips. Then she urged his head down over her belly and opened her legs. She laughed and moaned and stroked his hair as he nuzzled her. And he wasn't Russell Wheeler anymore. He was only her pleasure rising to the pressure of his lips and his tongue. Oh God, he thought. Oh God, oh God, oh God!

Then she urged him up, and she laughed as he entered

her, as if together they had rediscovered the most obvious secret. He felt her wetness as he lifted himself on his arms and her heels pressed into the small of his back. He felt himself falling, felt the smile on her face, the loss of gravity, the cries from her throat. My daughter, he thought. No. There was so much he wanted to say and nothing he could. He filled his mind with trees to make it last. Trees of New Guinea, trees of Labrador. But the trees faded to a bare plain from which her hips rose to meet him, her mouth open as if for a cry that didn't come. Thoughts dissolved in the hollow of her throat, the single diamond stud in her earlobe, her dark hair against the pillow, her elbows upturned, her hands grasping the spindles of the headboard. He was clinging to a ledge. The rock was beginning to crumble in his hands. His daughter. Dark angel surrounding him with her great dark wings.

He wondered how it had been with Nick. He tried to put this out of his mind. But still he wondered. Had there ever been this abandon? He knew there must have, as there had once been for him with Miriam so long ago and with others in their time, though it didn't matter. Lesley! Was this possible? A beginning or an aberration? This child, this daughter. He might've died in New Guinea. He might've died of a heart attack at the office, or in a car, or on a plane. He might never have known this. And how will she feel about it tomorrow, he wondered?

"Lesley." He began to speak.

"Don't," she said. "Don't say it."

IN NEW GUINEA HE HADN'T expected to survive. Only the moment had mattered—the sky at dawn or dusk, in the brief equatorial twilight when its beauty eclipsed the brutal heat of day and the shape-shifting chaos of the night. Now everything mattered so much, the here you can return to, the now you never can. He wished he could see his life as a movie or a play, feel the judgment of others and of himself as no more than images on a screen, or music, or shadows. He woke to see the glow of 6:00 on the digital clock on the bedside table. He lay there a minute, listening to the rain on the windows, wondering if he were waking from a memory or a dream. He couldn't recall Lesley's leaving. He smelled a trace of her perfume on the pillow and remembered the smell of her hair as he'd held her head in his hands. He buried his face in the pillow, heard a rustle of paper and then felt it under his hand. He switched on the bedside lamp and saw a piece of his own stationery, folded in half.

Dear Russell,
 No one else would understand. I don't think we quite understand it ourselves, so let's not try. I love you.
 P.S. There's fresh coffee in the kitchen.

27

Two weeks later, after it was generally known that Nick was gone and Lesley had filed for divorce, Russell began to receive phone calls from old friends of Miriam's, fishing for details. One of the callers was Mildred Wallace, who had tried to get something going with Russell after he and Miriam divorced. She had suggested they might console each other over their mutual loss of Miriam, but Russell hadn't felt a great need of consolation and had tried, with difficulty, to convey that to Mildred without seeming heartless. She brought him casseroles and invited him for quiet little dinners from which he made difficult and sometimes rather tactless retreats.

"People just don't seem willing to work at relationships anymore. Young people anyway."

Russell held the receiver with his shoulder and made a note on his calendar about an upcoming executive committee meeting. "Miriam and I weren't particularly young," he reminded her.

"Oh I didn't mean that. I didn't mean you. I'm talking about Nick and Lesley. It's just so sad."

"I don't know," Russell sighed. "Maybe it's best for them."

"But how are you Russell? I worry about you being alone so much."

"I'm doing all right. I see a lot of Lesley and Katy." He liked the idea that he was telling the truth.

"But you must be so disappointed in Nick. Just throwing away his future. Or so it seems."

"No, I'm not disappointed. Anyway, it's his life, isn't it?"

"Well yes, of course. I'm just concerned. I know how lonely it's been for me since Bill's been gone, and I know it's been hard for you without Miriam. I do miss her so. I just want you to know that I'm here for you when you need me, if you just want to talk, or anything."

Or anything? Russell smiled. "I appreciate that Mildred. It was kind of you to call."

MIRIAM HAD CALLED A WEEK earlier to tell him about her European tour and about meeting Princess Di and Sarah Ferguson at a reception. He listened and asked the appropriate questions about her impressions of the royal family and then told her that Nick had left Lesley and moved to New York.

"Oh," Miriam said, without much surprise in her voice. "What are people saying about it?"

"People?" Russell was a little bit stunned.

"Yes, people in town I mean."

"Well, they're saying it's too bad I guess, those that know about it. They're saying whatever they must've said about us when you left."

"When I left? Now you're being defensive."

"Defensive about what?"

"About everything. I just called to have a nice conversation, and you're spoiling it with recriminations."

"Well, I'm sorry then. I'm sorry I spoiled our nice conversation with all this talk about life on earth."

"Oh Russell . . ."

"Never mind."

"No, I'm sorry. I didn't mean to sound callous. I'm just not surprised. Whenever I've been with them they seemed so distant, as if they were just tolerating each other."

"Sound familiar?"

"Then you agree they're better off apart. How is Nicky handling it?"

"I don't know. I haven't heard from him. Have you?"

"No, of course not. I just wondered what he's doing."

"He's with a woman in New York. Her name's Philippa, and they're doing whatever people do there."

"Is she nice, this Philippa?"

"I don't know. I haven't met her."

"I just hope he's happy at least. I know Lesley wasn't much of a wife to him."

"Now how do you know that?"

"Oh Russell, I know these things. I'm not blind. I know when things aren't right."

"Yes, I guess you do. Well, Lesley and Katy are fine, in case you want to know."

"Yes, of course. Tell Lesley I'm sorry, and give little Katy a squeeze for me. I miss her so. Please."

"I will. I'll do that."

"You're a dear," she said. "Let me know anything you hear."

"I will." Russell put the receiver back on the cradle, then dropped the phone into one of the deep file drawers of his desk and closed it.

28

It thrilled russell to think that every now and then someone was killed and eaten by a bear, that there was still that kind of wildness in the country. It wasn't the kind of thought he expected anyone to understand, and of course he would feel sorry for the friends and family of whoever was eaten. But it reinforced the idea of the food chain as cyclic rather than linear, with man standing inviolate at the head of it. Every natural thing in the world had a purpose, if only to give itself up to foster something else. The rain giving itself to the grass, the grass to the deer, the deer to the hunter, the unfortunate hunter to the bear and the bear giving it all back to the soil in a mound of steaming dung. Better a man should be eaten by a bear than by war or disease or by his lack of will to go on living, a bear, to whom everything—man, fish, willow buds, berries—was fat for the long winter's sleep.

He remembered Jim Crowfoot, who was 106 when he died in his fishing boat on the lake in front of the house. Russell had come home from work one evening and seen him sitting, slumped over his rod as if he'd merely dozed off. Crowfoot had been a friend of Russell's father and grandfather and had spent every day of his life, as far back as Russell could remember, hunting, trapping or fishing on the lake. If I became eccentric enough, Russell thought, people would come to expect nothing from me. I could wear my clothes with the labels out. I could sit on a bench and feed the squirrels. Children would tug at my coat or pelt me with snowballs and I would laugh and pretend to chase them. He remembered how Crowfoot used to cover his bald spot by rubbing black shoe polish on his scalp and how, when he came to visit his father, Russell's dog Jupiter would bark and chew Jim's pant leg and Jim would only laugh and pet the dog affectionately and say, "It's okay. The poor things don't live very long."

Gravity held him to earth, and he had made miniscule changes in his world. But there were moments in which he gave up measuring himself, and in them his life became larger than he had envisioned it, no longer fettered by laws as mundane as Newton's or of supply and demand. In those moments he could be a star expanding and consuming itself over eons or a moth beating its life out against a window screen on a summer night.

29

"COFFEE?" TOM CAREY PUSHED the thermos across the table toward Russell. They had been joined by Paul Blakely, another member of the executive committee, as well as Gordon Smith, the company treasurer, and Taylor Stanley, the chief corporate counsel.

"No thanks," Russell passed the thermos along to Gordon. "I think I've had too much coffee already."

"We might as well get started," Tom said. "Art is out of town. Would you mind closing the door, Gordon?"

Tom leaned forward in his chair and clasped his manicured hands together on the table. The energy of his still youthful face was balanced by the graying of his dark brown hair. It feathered over his temples and gave him a benign leonine look. His bearing called no attention to itself and Russell only realized how extraordinarily erect his posture was when he saw him sitting or standing with others. As Russell observed him across the table it was easy to understand how Carey had so dramatically improved the performance of each department or division for which he had been responsible. Russell reflected on his recent conversation with Art Putney concerning Tom's effect on his co-workers. There was a fierce intelligence in Tom's gaze which, it seemed to Russell, could inspire or intimidate, depending upon one's willingness to meet it, and a clarity of enunciation in his voice which contrasted noticably with the predominant twang of those surrounding him.

"I've moved this meeting date forward because I think what we've learned can't wait." Tom looked at Russell as he spoke. "You're all aware of the unusual volume of our stock traded over the past few weeks and the jump in price from thirty to just over forty-two. We've been monitoring it, but we couldn't make out any pattern because of the use of street names in all the large transactions. We knew that Prudential Bache had bought up 164,000 shares at between thirty-two and thirty-eight, probably for arbitrage. We couldn't trace any pattern in the rest. But now we know that United Tobacco has accumulated over 800,000 shares."

"How did we learn this?" Russell asked.

"Taylor has a source at Lehman Brothers," Tom nodded toward Taylor Stanley.

"It's one of those things that gets overheard," Taylor said. "But this source is absolutely reliable."

"That's over ten percent of the shares outstanding," Russell observed.

"That's right," Tom said. "They'll have to file a declaration of intent with the SEC within ten days. But I don't think there's any question but that they're planning a takeover attempt."

"It makes sense," Paul scratched his head. "They've been looking for a non-tobacco leg."

"What's the current breakdown on our shareholders?" Russell asked, turning to Gordon Smith. "What've we got we can rely on?"

"About twenty-six percent we figure, in friendly hands," Gordon said. "Your family has just over ten, in aggregate, and another sixteen percent are held by the company, by local investors and by other long-term individual stockholders."

"And the rest?" Russell asked. "Institutional?"

"Pension funds, mutual funds," Gordon said, "Strictly market driven."

"And how much cash does United have?"

"We don't have any figures, but they've got a double A rating with Standard and Poors, and we do know that they've arranged a credit line of $500,000,000 with Chemical Bank."

"That should do it." Russell said. "What've we got to fight them with?"

"Our shareholder options," Taylor said, "our so-called poison pill program. It'll make us more expensive, but it won't stop them."

"You mean there really isn't anything we can do about it?" Russell asked. "If they want us badly enough, they can have us?"

"There's nothing we can do with dollars," Tom said. "We could try to buy up our own shares, but we'd lose if we got in a bidding war with United."

"What do our investment bankers say? I assume you talked with them."

"The same thing. Goldman figures United would be prepared to make a tender of sixty-five dollars a share."

"Holy shit!" Russell shifted in his chair as if he were preparing to get up and fight.

"They approached us earlier this year," Tom said. "I saw Larry DeMott, their chairman, at the NAM meeting in Cleveland. He told me that we were nice guys, and that they were nice guys, and that together we'd make one great company."

"If they're such nice guys they wouldn't be making a tender. Why didn't you tell us?" Russell demanded.

"I didn't even want to talk to him. I just told him we weren't interested. I didn't want to risk putting us in play."

"But you should've let me know," Russell insisted.

"I'm sorry, Russ," Tom gestured. "I knew you'd be against it. I just didn't want to bother you with what I thought was only a fishing expedition."

"I appreciate your consideration, but something like this is worth being bothered about."

"I'm sorry. I should have told you."

"Okay." Russell sighed heavily. "So what are we going to do?"

"Taylor has an idea," Tom said.

"An antitrust suit," Taylor said. "It's a long shot on the face of it, but I think it's worth a try. United has Delta Paper, a wholly-owned subsidiary, that manufactures its cigarette papers, packs and cartons. It's not a major part of their business, but they also sell labels and packaging material to a few private label food companies, and the right judge might look at their attempt to acquire us, with our Carter Label division, as an act in restraint of trade. It's enough to file a suit on anyway, and it would tie their bid up in court for a while. They might even get discouraged and go after someone else."

"Unlikely," Tom said.

"It's worth a shot," Russell said. "It'll buy us some time."

ON HIS WAY OUT, AS RUSSELL stopped to speak with Madge Long, his old secretary, Tom called to him from the door of his office. "You going down Russ?"

"Yes."

"Just a minute and I'll walk out with you."

They said good night to the receptionist and walked to the reserved spaces where their cars were parked.

"I just wanted to tell you I was sorry to hear about Nick." Tom said. "I wish I could've been more help to him."

"Thank you, Tom. I appreciate that." Russell turned toward his car.

"I've wanted to ask you something." Tom called out, and they paused in front of Tom's BMW. It irritated Russell that Tom didn't drive a Detroit car, but he had vowed that he wouldn't make an issue of it.

"I know it's quite soon after the separation," Tom said, "and I don't know how you might feel about it, but I'm chairman of the Muscular Dystrophy Society and I need a date, a partner for our Christmas dance at the Grand Rapids Hilton. I wondered if you'd have any objection if I invited Lesley to go with me. I thought it might cheer her up to get out."

"Lesley? No." Russell cleared his throat. "Excuse me. No. I wouldn't object. It'd be up to Lesley, of course."

"Of course," Tom echoed. He put his hand on Russell's shoulder. "Are you all right?"

"Yes." Russell coughed again and wiped the tears that had come to his eyes. "Just a bug. I'm getting over it." He turned toward his Buick.

"Well, thank you, Russ. I've always admired Lesley, but I didn't know how you might feel about it."

"Good night." Russell's voice was raspy. He started his car and watched as Tom backed out his BMW and drove toward the street. What would he have thought if I'd said no, Russell wondered.

30

"What does all this mean?" Lesley asked. They were sitting in the living room of her house overlooking Big Bear Lake. Floodlights from the house illuminated the new snow, and they could see glass-like panes of ice suspended in the reeds along the edge of the water. They had taken Katy to one of the company pine plantings to select a Christmas tree, and after dinner they had decorated it with ten strings of lights, tinsel, and almost two hundred ornaments and played five games of Old Maid with her before she could be convinced that it was time for bed. Lesley fixed Russell a third bourbon and water, switched off the tape of Gene Autry singing "Rudolph the Red-Nosed Reindeer" and plugged an Oscar Peterson disc in the CD player behind the couch.

"It means," Russell said, taking a careful first sip from the overfull glass, "that if we can't stop them, those bastards will probably make Five Oaks into a ghost town."

"But in the papers they said that they didn't intend to make any changes." She leaned back against an arm of the couch and stretched her legs across Russell's lap.

"If they weren't going to make any changes, they wouldn't be making the move. There's got to be some leverage to make it worth their while. In our case, they'd probably move corporate headquarters to Richmond and close down the Five Oaks Mill all together."

"Because it's inefficient?"

"It's outdated. This isn't exactly the hub of commerce. We're here because this is where we got started."

"So the employees would just be out on the streets."

"They might transfer a few technical people to other locations, and they'd move a few key executives to Richmond. Most of our stock is held by institutions, banks and mutual funds, and they won't pass up a chance to make a quick fifty percent profit. Most of our long-term stockholders don't want to sell. I don't want to sell."

"Do you think the lawsuit will work?" She rested her arm on the back of the couch and massaged Russell's shoulder.

"I don't know. I'd like to settle it with tire irons. I hate the idea that those sons of bitches can come in here and crush the life out of this town. They don't think about people, or if they do, they don't care. Maybe I'm just getting too old."

"You just care more than most people." She rubbed his neck.

"No I don't. At least I hope I don't." Russell was quiet for a minute. He massaged Lesley's feet, and he smiled at her. "It's nice to hear this music," he said.

"And Gene Autry?"

"Yes, and Gene Autry," he laughed. "Though I can do without that for another year at least. I was afraid we wouldn't have much to talk about."

"We always have."

"I know," Russell said, "but it's different now."

"Why?"

"It's hard for me to believe you aren't just being kind."

"Maybe I am." Lesley smiled.

"But why? Why me?"

"I have a woman's reasons."

Russell took her head in his hands.

"I think what I liked most about Nick," she said, "was the thought that he might grow up to be you."

"That makes me sad." Russell dropped his hands to her shoulders.

"What makes you sad?"

"Nick. I can't help feeling I'm betraying him."

"Oh Russell, stop it!" She dug her thumbs into his shoulders. "Nick cut himself off. From you, from me, from Katy. He was a weak person, that's all. He was jealous of you, jealous of Katy. You can't go on making excuses for him."

31

For several years Russell had tracked the approaching solstice. He noted each day where the sun rose, on those days it was visible, and thought to himself that that spot, just to the right of the tallest white pines across the road, was as far south as it would go. No matter how dark the winter might seem, once the sun reached that point the days would be getting longer and the sun would be, however imperceptibly, climbing back toward the crown of the sky. Several times he commented to Lesley that as he grew older he felt a greater need for sunlight. In just three weeks he could begin tracking the lengthening hours with a book of climatic charts and savoring each additional minute of light as if it were a personal achievement. He had always felt that those retired people who wintered in Florida had somehow given up on real life and settled for a manufactured substitute, as if, having visited the Chinese Pavillion, they believed they'd been to China.

But Russell was beginning to understand the efficacy of substitutes. He couldn't abide the "Ain't We Got Fun," waiting-for-the-Grim-Reaper passivity of Florida. But there might be other places, real places, where the sun shone and a man could feel he was living an actual life. That mountainside above the Gila Valley. But that might be too much to live with every day, too much for the imagination. He knew he could only take beauty in small doses or he became numb to it. Maybe such grandeur should only be glimpsed from the corner of the eye. He remembered one morning, near the end of a too long vacation with Miriam, standing on their balcony over the ultramarine Caribbean and longing for the gray March landscape of Five Oaks. Maybe life would be easier if they went to live somewhere they weren't known. But Katy needed a settled life. And what would she think of them as she grew older? He made a quick calculation. He would be eighty-one when she graduated from high school.

No matter how much old music Lesley listened to or how many old movies she saw, it could only be the kind of experience one gathers from a museum, and she was sure to become bored as the curator of his past. She needs memories of her own time, he thought. And he thought how little future there was for him, just enough to make her a widow past her prime.

Lately he had felt abnormally fatigued. He wondered if it might be a mild virus or simply the combined strain of Nick's leaving and the threat of a takeover. There was some stiffness in his legs and shoulders, but otherwise he felt as fit as he ever had. He remembered something his father had said shortly before he went into the hospital that final time, that an old man didn't feel like an old man but simply like a young man with something wrong.

It would only take one bright February day to set him right, one still, clear day when the chickadees would begin their spring song again and the sky above the snow would be so blue you could swim in it, a day you could feel the heat of the sun on your face through the frost of your own breath. One clear day, if he could survive the darkness of January. How many more days like that might there be, and how many such days had he wasted, struggling for some achievement he might bask in, though he'd long ago lost any talent for basking.

32

In the forty-odd years since the war, Lesley was the only person Russell had told how he felt when he first heard the engine of the plane that eventually came to rescue him, a harsher, more articulated sound than any he had heard since the day of his crash on the ridge above Tapua, and how often he'd wondered what might've become of him if it hadn't appeared that day over the clearing.

He hadn't been happy living with the People, not as he had always thought of happiness—getting what he wanted or thought he wanted, however ephemeral. In Tapua there was nothing to want. He hadn't known love there, certainly not romantic love, but he had felt adoration from the People, and affection for them. He hadn't been able to accept the women who had come to him as if to a god, coated in pig grease and ceremonial white mud. Only in the last few months before the plane had he taken one of them, or, more accurately, allowed one of them to take him. Kopa ki's third wife, Kantu, was only a girl with budding breasts and he'd often wondered, in the years since, if a child had come of it.

Once he accepted the life of Tapua as the only life there was or would be, he had known a kind of peace, a self-sustaining animal existence without attachment to life or concern for death. He did what he could for the People as an emissary from another time, bringing to the Stone Age what spotty knowledge he possessed of medicine or sanitation or invention, though their ignorance and superstition permitted them to accept little of it.

The droning of the plane came to him more as a troubling feeling than as a sound, the queasiness of an implacable memory rising, a face without a name. His first impulse had been to hide from it, like Adam in the garden, though Tapua was hardly Eden. He felt the discrete explosions of its engine against his skin, as palpable a sound as when he had first heard the split-log drums pounding out an insult to a neighboring tribe or the screams of an enemy captive forced to watch his limbs being severed and eaten before his own eyes. He observed its first pass from the shadow of a pandamus tree, saw the silver glint of the sun off its wings and dropped the pointed stick with which he'd been planting sweet potatos. The People scattered in a confusion of fear and excitement, much as he had felt, though for different reasons. Was it a messenger from the Land of the Dead, or was it the God of the Sky bringing his long promised gifts to them? He watched the tiny people with huge savage faces run into the clearing waving their arms, then lose courage again and dive under the stilt-supported floors of their houses. Airplane. The word came to him with images of cars, ships, fire and mass destruction, white women, concrete sidewalks, books, electric lights and the shapes of once familiar trees. Airplane.

It was a high-winged plane without military insignia. He wondered if the Japs had planes like that. He watched it climb out, watched the tribesmen scatter like blown leaves in its wake, watched it circle and drop below the ridge of the near mountains for another pass. The plane was so vivid against the green slope he suddenly felt drawn to it, not by any considered thought but as if by an instinct. He found himself running into the clearing, felt his arms spread wide in greeting as it swooped down again, so low he could see that the pilot was wearing sunglasses. He'd forgotten about sunglasses. He saw the wings waggle as the plane climbed out, then leveled and grew distant until he thought it was gone. But it banked, turned back, then dove and came straight at him until he suspected it might be going to strafe.

Then something crashed into the thatch of Kopa ki's house. The plane pulled up, dipped its wings and climbed out over the ridge of the far mountains.

Russell ran to the hut and saw Kopa ki's feet shuffling for balance on an overhead beam as he worked to free from the thatch whatever the plane had dropped.

"Look Quari," Kopa ki shouted, "Look! Your father from the sky has sent a gift." He crouched on the beam and handed down something wrapped in a small bundle of white canvas. Russell took it and in the process of upwrapping it recognized, from the feel of it, that it was a beer bottle. God, a beer bottle! He'd forgotten there were such miraculous things, and would later reflect that, at that moment, it probably held more magic for him than it had for Kopa ki.

"Yes, it is a gift!" Russell said. He removed the wrapping paper and saw that it was a torn piece of a map and that there was a message scribbled on it in pencil:

If you are a white man and can read this, make a mark on the ground in the shape of a cross on the slope below the village. I'll be back in two or three days.

"It's a sign," Russell said, "from my father in the sky. He asks for a sign in return."

"How do you know, Quari?" Kopa ki asked.

"I am from the sky," Russell said solemnly, "and I know such things."

"Forgive me Quari." Kopa ki looked away. Then he turned back toward Russell, and his eyes grew wide. "Does this mean the sky god will bring us more gifts?"

"Possibly," Russell nodded. "But we must do as he says or he will be angry."

"What about this?" Kopa ki held up the beer bottle. "What is its magic?"

"It has two magics," Russell said. "You can see."

"Ah!" Kopa ki exclaimed. He held the bottle up to the sunlight and rotated it in his hand. "It is filled with green light," he said. "I have never seen anything like this. It is like a piece of the sky I can hold in my hand."

"Yes," Russell nodded, "a piece of the sky."

"And its other magic?" Kopa ki asked.

Russell took the bottle from him and placed it to his lips and blew.

"The voice of the sky?" Kopa ki blew into it, "It has a funny little voice." He blew into it again, then held it up and examined it in the light of the sun.

RUSSELL WATCHED SKEPTICALLY for the plane's return, and if it hadn't been for the beer bottle which Kopa Ki fondled and tooted almost incessantly, and for the message on the torn map in a hand not his own, he might have believed he'd only dreamt of its appearance. But by the time he again heard the faint droning three days later, a cross had been constructed from two casuarina logs of unequal length, bound with a twine of twisted kunai grass and white-washed with a mixture of grease, mud and ashes. On its second pass over the village, the plane dropped a parachute attached to a canvas pack which contained four machetes, an orange windsock, a set of instructions and specifications for constructing a landing strip, and a hand-drawn map indicating its location in the valley below. The pack also contained a compass, a box of Hersey bars, a carton of Camel cigarettes and another note, this one typed:

> When you've finished clearing the strip, put the windsock up near the north end of it (compass provided), and make it as smooth as you can. My life and your's may depend on it. I'll be back in a fortnight, weather permitting.

The note was signed, "Lloyd Auken," in the same hand in which the first note had been written.

The following weeks seemed as long as all the previous time he had spent in Tapua. He told Kopa ki that the great bird needed an altar on which to land and, using the drawing dropped by Lloyd Auken, explained how they would use the machetes to clear it. Kopa ki oversaw the clearing, gesturing with and blowing on the beer bottle as a symbol of his authority and of the promise of what the God of the Sky would bring to them through his great, raucous, frightening bird.

33

IN THEIR UPPER WEST SIDE APARTMENT, Philippa brought
Nick a cup of black coffee and put it on the desk where he
was sorting through boxes of papers and photographs Lesley had packed up and sent to him.

"I want you to have all these," she had written. "I don't
want them around like a ghost in the closet."

He untied the strings of an accordion file-folder and
pulled out a photo of his father with a pump-action shotgun
tucked under his arm, and Bing, their black Labrador, sitting eagerly beside him with his tongue hanging out. The
picture had been taken beside a barn somewhere near Five
Oakes and reminded Nick of an afternoon in late summer
when he was twelve and about to enter the seventh grade.
His father had been explaining the safe handling of firearms
as they drove to a field behind the house on his grandfather's
farm. They had that same pump shotgun, a hand trap and a
case of clay pigeons.

"You're going to be in junior high this year," his father
was saying as the old pick-up jounced over the ruts in the
two-track. "Getting on in the world. I guess I was hunting
by the time I was ten."

Nick had never fired a gun or even actually heard one at
close range. He had listened to his father's hunting stories
and seen the beautiful dead pheasants on the basement floor.
He had smelled the rich, sour odor of their ripening flesh
and he collected their tail feathers and occasionally bit down
on a piece of number six shot while chewing a mouthful of
breast meat. But the process by which they came to be so
beautifully dead was a mystery. His father demonstrated

the loading procedure, the pump action of the forearm grip, the use of the safety and emphasized again that never under any circumstances should he let the barrel point in the direction of another person.

"There's no such thing as an unloaded gun," Russell reiterated. "You're always hearing about some poor son of a bitch getting blown away with a gun some other damn fool didn't think was loaded."

His father showed him how to pitch the disc-shaped ceramic targets with the hand trap, demonstrated the shouldering and swing of the gun and explained about sighting the barrel under the bird and following the rise of it. He had Nick pitch a few birds out over the dry grass so he could see how they flew. Then he loaded the gun, glanced over at Nick and hollered, "Pull."

Nick made the throwing motion and the spring-arm of the trap flung the small yellow disc in as ascending arc toward the trees. It sailed perfectly and then disintegrated in a puff of black dust. The blast of the gun was unimaginably loud and hit Nick like a shock wave. A prickly sensation skittered through his scalp. Guns in the movies had never been that loud. It was a vicious, ripping sound that echoed off the distant barn and came back to them from the trees of the woodlot. His father's shoulder had jerked back and the long black barrel jumped toward the sky. His father racked the slide handle back and a green plastic shell casing spun to the ground and lay smoking in the sand of the road at his feet.

Nick swallowed deliberately and thought that maybe he didn't want to learn hunting after all. His father powdered two more clay birds before offering the gun to Nick in exchange for the trap.

"That's okay," Nick said. "I don't think I really want to try it right now."

"But we're here now, Nick." His father's voice was edged with impatience.

"I just don't want to."

"Are you scared of it?" his father prodded.

"No." Nick lied.

"You've got to do things that scare you sometimes," his father insisted. "Everything new is scary at first. If you don't do it now you probably never will."

Nick took the gun reluctantly. It seemed heavier than it had before he had seen the flash from the muzzle and heard its bark. He felt the heat of the barrel in his hands. "Is it loaded?" he asked.

"No," his father replied, "but you always have to assume that it is. Remember?"

Nick thought of the gun as a wild animal he had been handed, one that might turn on him at any moment. He asked his father again about the safety. His father held out three shells. "Now press those into the loading gate like I showed you."

Nick took the shells and worked them gingerly against the shiny steel breechblock. He expected the mechanism to snap out and mutilate his thumb. His father reminded him to check the safety. "Now pump a shell into the chamber," he coached.

Nick pumped it, and the forearm slid back into place with alarming precision, as if it had a mind of its own.

"Ready when you are," his father said. His arm was cocked back behind his shoulder.

Nick wasn't thinking about the target or about anything his father had told him. He was thinking only about the blast, the recoil and the heat of the exploding shell. He concentrated on keeping his cheek clear of the black metal receiver. He tried to swallow but couldn't. He couldn't breathe. He prayed he wouldn't lose his grip when the gun went off. He pushed the safety button, and it turned red.

"Pull," he croaked weakly.

He heard the motion of his father's arm, heard the trap spring the target into flight, but he wasn't watching it. He closed his eyes and jerked at the trigger. It was over before it began. Somehow the noise hadn't been as loud as when his father had fired it. It hadn't really been frightening at all and the kick had been no more of a jolt than he might have gotten from one of his friends punching him on the shoulder at school.

"That bird's safe," his father laughed. "Don't forget to pump it."

Nick felt he had conquered something. He fired twice more and reloaded. He was keeping his eyes open now, watching the target, and on his fourth shot he powdered it. "Bingo!" his father cried. "Dead on."

Nick took a dozen more birds and powdered or fractured at least half of them. The gun seemed to have shrunk considerably. It felt almost like a toy in his hands. He reloaded again and powdered another one.

"Just a minute," his father called. "I have to get some more birds."

Nick turned toward him as he spoke and unconsciously pumped the forearm. There was a sudden explosion and the gun bucked in Nick's hands.

Russell stood frozen, reaching toward the case of targets, in the odd, hunched position he had been in when the earth jumped around him and the sand sprayed up at his feet. "Jesus Christ!" he screamed. He turned slowly toward Nick and it was as if all the expression had been blown off his face. His eyes were black dots of anger and shock. The gun had tricked him, Nick thought. Just as he had come to trust it, it had gone off on its own. His father took two violent steps and grabbed the gun from his hands.

"I didn't do anything," Nick protested numbly. "It just went off by itself."

His father racked the pump arm several times, rapidly, and one spent shell and one live one flew to the ground. Then he walked purposefully to the truck, slid the gun into its soft leather case on the seat and zipped it up.

Nick felt he had been betrayed somehow. He looked out the window as his father drove. Row by row, even the tasselled corn seemed to be condemning him. They rode in silence all the way to the farmhouse, then past the farmhouse, all the way to the edge of town. Finally he heard his father clear his throat. "You'll get the hang of it," he said.

"We'll try it again and you'll remember everything I told you." They turned up Tyler Street at the corner by the high school. "And then one of these days we'll try hunting together," his father said.

At the dinner table his mother asked how the shooting lesson had gone.

"Fine. Just fine," his father said.

Nick wanted to tell his mother and Marlis about the clay pigeons he had shattered, powdered "dead on," but it was better to leave it at "fine," he thought, better not to have to explain to them how he had almost blown his father's legs off. "Fine," his father had said. Then he had gone on to talk about his upcoming trip to Chicago, about the banquet at which he was to be honored by the National Association of Manufacturers, and the subject of guns or hunting never came up between them again.

NICK SLID THE PHOTOGRAPH back into the file and retied the strings. He put the file back into the packing case and carried it to the closet in the alcove off the hall. He would sort through it all some other day, he thought. The box fit perfectly under the bottom shelf in the closet. He slid it back in the corner against the wall and closed the door.

34

Russell's annual early december cocktail party was a highlight of the Five Oaks holiday season. Apart from a few small dinners, it had been the only entertaining he had done at home since his divorce, and invitations were coveted. The guest list was limited to close friends, company executives known personally to Russell and occasional newcomers whose acquaintance Russell had recently made. This year Lesley had suggested a few new people to be invited and had volunteered to act as hostess.

The din of conversation and laughter made a music more audible than the tapes Lesley had selected to promote a festive mood. The guests looked as bright and polished as the silver chafing dishes on the buffet. The lintels were draped with lighted boughs of imitation holly. And as if it had been ordered to complement the scene, a downy and windless snow was falling.

Lesley's long auburn hair was folded back on one side with a diamond barrette. Her black knit dress was accented by a red velvet bow pinned to her shoulder and a single strand of pearls. She offered a tray of caviar and onion canapes to Art and Phyllis Putney.

"She's still a beautiful young woman," Mildred Wallace observed. She was standing with Russell by the fireplace, watching Lesley across the room. Russell wished she hadn't made it sound like an indictment.

"Has she decided what she's going to do, after the divorce? I mean there just isn't much for a single woman in Five Oaks. I should know."

Another indictment? Russell wondered. "She still has her job," he replied.

Now Lesley offered the canapes to Tom Carey, and Tom was saying something to her, leaning close to her ear as if sharing a secret. And Lesley smiled and blushed and appeared to whisper something to Tom. Russell noticed how the people in Tom's vicinity, those who were engaged in their own conversations, stood half-turned toward him somewhat deferentially, as if hoping he might speak to them. These weren't only the company people, Russell observed. Even Warren Riorden had volunteered, having just met Tom, that he felt Russell had done an excellent job in selecting his successor. "A throughly engaging fellow," Warren had said. Russell thought of how he would like to walk over to that corner of the room, take Lesley in his arms and kiss her, long and hard, right in front of Tom and everybody. He imagined how Mildred might react to this, and smiled broadly.

"What on earth is so funny?" Mildred inquired.

"What?" Russell came up short. "I'm sorry, Mildred, what did you say?"

"I asked what you thought was so funny. You just started grinning for no apparent reason."

"Oh did I? I'm sorry, Mildred. I was just thinking how right you are. About her being beautiful I mean."

"And that's why you smiled so idiotically?"

"Yes. I smile about things like that all the time."

"Well you looked positively lecherous. Not that it was unbecoming." Mildred raised her eyebrows. "But I worry about you, Russell. I really do."

"I know, and I appreciate that. It's just that it's Christmas, and I'm happy, and I feel like smiling."

Mildred batted her eyes at the panelled ceiling. "I think you're getting old. You're getting more eccentric, anyway."

"Well thank you, Mildred." Russell smiled. "I've always wanted to be eccentric." He excused himself and walked over to the buffet to greet Paul and Eunice Blakely. He noticed that Lesley was still talking with Tom and that Tom was standing close, resting his hand on the bookshelf behind her. It looked as if he had her hemmed in, and Lesley was laughing.

AFTER THE LAST GUESTS had departed, Russell found a couple of stray glasses on his desk, picked them up and wiped the residual rings of moisture with a Kleenex. He felt buoyed up by the good spirits of the party and the confirmation that many people still held him in high regard. A few of his guests had expressed their sympathy about Nick's departure and some pointedly avoided it, but most were concerned about the threatened takeover and asked questions Russell could answer only with guarded speculation.

His house felt good to him again, and it was possible for him to think that it was really Christmas. He wished Marlis was coming home, but she had explained to him that she couldn't come without Elizabeth, and she wasn't quite ready to expose Elizabeth to Five Oaks and vice versa.

He carried the glasses to the kitchen. Lesley was finishing the dishes, as Josephine had left early for her Women's Fellowship dinner at the Methodist church.

"Two more," Russell said, setting the glasses on the counter by the sink.

"Thanks." Lesley smiled over her shoulder. "I was afraid I might be finished."

"It's fun playing house with you." He wrapped his arms around her ribs and kissed the back of her neck.

She leaned back into his embrace, her hands still immersed in the dishwater. "How do you think it went?"

"No one got too drunk or broke anything." Snow was still falling steadily, and Russell watched it through the window as he spoke. "And no one went away mad, as far as I know."

"Did anyone say anything? About Nick, I mean?"

"Mildred Wallace is concerned about your potential social life, or the lack of it."

"Mildred is concerned about *your* social life." Lesley

dried her hands on a dish towel as she turned away from the sink.

Russell took the towel from her and kissed her. "I've wanted to do that all evening, right in front of God and everybody."

"I don't think anyone would've noticed, or cared."

He touched his forehead to hers. "Most of those people would be shocked." He paused. "They'd think I was a monster."

"Probably."

"It'd be the juiciest thing since Linus Brooks ran off with his wife's sister."

"Linus Brooks came back, and no one even thinks about it anymore."

"That's true," Russell conceded. He slid his hands down to her hipbones and held her firmly against him. "But Linus wasn't robbing the cradle. Linus wasn't an old man."

"Do you think of yourself as an old man?" Lesley turned toward him.

"No. But I'll be sixty-seven years old, and you're . . ."

"Thirty-seven."

"Do you want to spend your middle age watching me grow feeble and irascible? I can't have more than ten or fifteen good years."

"I could have an accident tomorrow," Lesley said. "I could die of cancer." She kissed him on the forehead. In her heels, she was almost exactly his height. She kissed him lightly on the lips. She let her hand fall between them and felt him stiffen. "I think you like me," she whispered.

He brushed his face against her hair. "I like your tricks," he murmured. "Maybe you'd like to show me more of them."

She nibbled his earlobe. "Maybe I would," she said.

THE HEMLOCKS SURROUNDING the bedroom windows were lit by outdoor floodlights, and the powdery snow piling up on their branches cast a soft light into the room. They lay in bed watching the brilliant flakes falling. Lesley leaned across Russell's chest to see the clock on the nightstand.

"Mmmm," he groaned, "I thought I felt fairies dancing on my chest."

"Mammary glands," she corrected.

"Even better," he smiled. "Dancing mammaries."

"I told the sitter I'd be home by midnight."

"It's a Saturday night." Russell reminded her.

"Tom Carey asked me out," Lesley announced abruptly, "to go to some charity ball with him."

"What did you tell him?"

"I said I'd let him know."

"He's an attractive guy."

"Yes, he is."

"Maybe you should. You'd probably have a good time. You'd meet some new people."

"Maybe I will."

"I'm trying not to be selfish about it. I don't want what I want to spoil your life."

"Good. Now can we stop talking about it?" Lesley sat up and held the bedcovers to her breast. "I had a letter from Nick," she said.

"What did he say? Why didn't you tell me?"

"I didn't want to talk about it before the party. He wrote about the settlement. He said I could have the house and half of everything else."

"You don't need anything else. You don't even need the house. You can have this one."

"I can't tell Nick that," she said.

Russell buried his face in her hair. "I love the smell of you," he said. "I'd like to spend the rest of my life just smelling you."

"He said he hadn't written to you because he hasn't known what to say," Lesley continued, ignoring Russell's nuzzling. "He's taking some courses in small business management at N.Y.U. He and Philippa are opening an antiques store on the Upper West Side."

"Antiques?" Russell sat up.

"Uh huh," Lesley nodded.

"I never knew he was interested in antiques." Nick's plans weren't what he really wanted to discuss.

"Philippa is," Lesley said. "She works for Christie's. I think he's likely to take on a whole range of new interests, though he always did like to collect strange things, old compasses and telescopes and sextants, and old guns. Mostly nautical stuff. He enclosed a list of things like that to send him with his clothes."

AFTER LESLEY LEFT, RUSSELL lay awake thinking. He wondered how much of Nick's failure had been his fault, or if he should even think of it as a failure. What was it that had kept Nick from loving Lesley and Katy? Selfishness? Russell felt his anger rising. What's left for me? I gave him a life and he refused it. Maybe he's incapable of appreciating anything.

Russell sat up and looked out the window. The snow flashing by in the floodlights had a mesmerizing effect. Wasn't there some proverb, he wondered, about the son having to go out and seek something the father never found, and that if the father had found it, the son would be denied that possibility in his own life? Was that what it was to be born dead, to have the end given to you at the beginning? Or did it only mean the son had to seek in another direction?

When Russell got up to switch off the floodlights, the snow had finally stopped falling.

35

Only once during his years in Tapua had Russell felt threatened by the deification that had been his aegis. On the third night of an unrelentingly violent thunderstorm, following a near-total eclipse of the sun, Kapoua, Neggi's half-brother, began to chatter about how the God of the Sky was angry with the People for keeping his son prisoner. He proposed that Russell should be made to fly from the lip of the gorge above the river; that only by returning him to the sky would the God be appeased and the life of the village spared. "These arrows of fire are his spears," Kapoua warned. "God is shaking them at us."

"Kapoua is full of bana becaue Quari is my friend." Kopa ki thrust out his chin as he spoke. "If his father was angry, Quari would tell us. If he wanted his son back, he would take him. He is the God, not Kapoua."

While the storm raged, the other men in the Spirit House would not meet Russell's gaze. They sat or lay trance-like, their eyes seeking the darkness out of which the thunder came and through which the lightning crazed the sky. But Kopa ki wore six tusk-bracelets on his arms; more than any other man in the village, and once he had spoken in Russell's defense, no one would challenge him.

The following morning, when a pellucid blue dome spanned the mountains surrounding the village, Kapoua himself was launched from the rim of the escarpment and failed to gain any altitude at all. His body shrank to the size of a fire ant before dissolving into the shadows of the canyon. It made no visible splash in the river and, though they listened carefully, sent back to them no sound at all.

36

For months Russell hadn't paid any attention to the painting on the wall by his closet, but this morning his eye had been drawn to it upon first waking, and he carried its image in and out of sleep. Several times he resisted the impulse, forged through years of discipline, to swing his feet immediately to the floor, and instead indulged what he knew to be a perilous practice so early in the morning: thinking about his life.

"When you wake up, get up, and when you get up, stay awake," had been his father's adage for success. Russell knew the dizzying gestalt posed by daydreaming, one stray thought careening off another until he was hardly aware he was living on earth.

In the somber winter light, the painting was for the first time charged with a peculiar resonance: a landed sailboat, aslant on its keel at the edge of a snow-covered field of corn stubble. Perhaps it was because no plan of action occurred to him as he lay contemplating the day; he had no appointments, no errands to run, no book currently engaging his interest. He would not, on principle, allow himself to watch daytime television. He might put on a suit and go down to the office, but even that failed to interest him, and he knew Tom Carey would resent an unbidden appearance. It was in this uneasy mood that he hatched a plan, a course of action which seemed too obvious to be ignored.

As soon as Lesley answered the phone, Russell announced that he was going to New York.

"When?"

"This afternoon."

"Why?"

"I've decided I have to talk to Nick."

"Do you think it's a good idea?"

"It's not an idea. I have to do it. Do you want to come with me? It'd just be a couple of days."

"To talk to Nick?" Lesley gasped.

"No. Just to be with me."

"I'd love it! If I can find someone to cover for me at the office and someone to stay with Katy. But it's only two weeks till Christmas. What about plane reservations and hotels?"

"We'll take the company plane, and I'll pull some strings. I think I still have some clout."

A LIMOUSINE FROM THE CARLYLE was waiting for them at La Guardia, a liveried driver nearby holding up a cardboard sign.

Marlis was still reeling with surprise when Russell began to explain his mission. "After your last visit, I guess I should expect you just about anytime," she laughed. "The new impulsive Russell B. Wheeler. Did you come to spend Christmas?" They were seated on the couch and Marlis had fixed herself a drink, though Russell had declined.

"No," Russell smiled sheepishly. He was sitting on the edge of the cushion as if, at any moment, he might spring to his feet. "How's Elizabeth?" he asked.

"She's had a bit of a rash, poor dear. It has something to do with the weather. It's nothing serious. She's out buying me a Christmas present I think. She'll be sorry she wasn't here; she took quite a shine to you. Any chance you could join us for dinner?"

Russell stacked the coasters on the table. "No, I don't think so." He picked a piece of lint off the sleeve of his sportcoat. "I'd like to, but I'm only in town till tomorrow. I came to talk to you about something, and to talk to Nick if he'll see me."

"Sounds pretty mysterious," Marlis said. "I can't wait to

hear what it is." She patted his hand. "Go ahead," she urged him.

"The last time I came to see you," he began diffidently, "you kind of dropped a bombshell on me."

"Yes I did," Marlis laughed, "and I must say you took it beautifully."

"Well," Russell cleared his throat, "now I've got one to drop on you."

"Really?" Marlis arched her eyebrows and laughed.

"It's not anything bad," he hedged. "At least I don't think it is."

"Dad, get to the point." She put her hand on his knee.

"Okay. Here it is." He swallowed audibly. "I've been seeing Lesley. I mean in more than just a friendly way." He felt a wave of heat cross his face.

"Really?" Marlis laughed. "Do you mean that you've become lovers?"

"Yes," he said. "I mean we're in love. At least I'm in love with her."

"You old cradle robber," Marlis chided.

"Are you shocked?"

"No, not really. I'm a little surprised." She smiled her knowing smile. "I didn't think you could let up on that tight rein of yours. But I'm not shocked."

"Oh!" Russell seemed almost disappointed.

"Is this serious?"

"It is for me," he shrugged. "You know me."

"Yes I do." Marlis leaned back against the bolster of the couch and folded her hands across her lap. "And what about Lesley? Is she serious?"

"I know she cares for me."

"I'm sure she does." Marlis dipped her head and regarded him over the rims of her glasses. "But is it love or just refuge? Are you setting yourself up for a heartbreak?"

"Refuge?"

"Security. Comfort. A shoulder to lean on."

"Well, that too, I'm sure. It seems funny, our talking about it like this." Russell smiled nervously.

"Are you asking me for advice?"

"I don't know. Do you have any?"

"Don't tell Nick about it." She leaned forward. "There's no reason to. I mean you're not talking about marriage or anything are you?"

"No." Russell shook his head. "But I love her. I feel dishonest somehow."

"That's your false sense of nobility again. I think you ought to try to control it."

"Maybe I won't tell him, but I can't leave it this way. I at least have to talk to him. He's still my son." He grasped Marlis's hand. "Will you call him for me?"

"Of course I will, but I'm not endorsing the idea." She excused herself and went into the bedroom to make the call.

Russell walked across the room and read the framed award certificates Marlis had received for her public relations work. He studied the photographs in the hall, Marlis in rolled up jeans, her saddle shoes dangling over the edge of the red velvet sofa which had stood at the foot of his and Miriam's bed. She held an infant Nick in her arms, and her smile was punctuated with a missing tooth. Nick in his uniform, just back from Viet Nam; Nick and Lesley's wedding, with Marlis as a bridesmaid; a Christmas card photo of himself at the wheel of a lift-truck, hoisting a smiling Marlis and Nick and an uneasy looking Miriam up in a crate toward the camera; Marlis in a mortarboard at her graduation from Smith; a sepia-toned photo of him and Miriam on their wedding day, standing by his father's 1937 Ford in front of the old Methodist church, about to leave on their honeymoon drive to the Straits of Mackinac.

He looked up as he heard Marlis returning.

"He said okay."

"Okay? How did he say it?"

"Just okay," Marlis shrugged.

AS THE CAB HURTLED AND splashed its way toward the West Side, Russell caught himself rehearsing his presentation to Nick and struggled to refocus his attention on the present.

The park looked . . . what was the word? Grimy, he decided, or withered. The rain-dark trees floated in fog above
the soupy vestiges of snow like wartime photographs of
Europe. As you know, Lesley and I have . . . no. Lesley was
devastated by your leaving, and I . . . DeAngello, Mario
DeAngello, 432491. Confession is good for the soul, he
thought. He read the driver's name and number off the per-
mit on the dash and began committing it to memory for no
good reason.

Nick turned from the window, plunged his hands into his
pockets and walked the length of the room. He paused a
moment, staring at the baseboard heater, then paced back
to his desk and sat on a corner of it. It was the third time he
had been to the window since Marlis's call, and he was angry with himself for being nervous. He had felt quite independent the past several months, and now a single phone
call made him feel once again that he had been called to the
woodshed. I won't listen, he thought. I'll let him talk but
I'm not going back to Five Oaks.

It wasn't that Russell had ever been harsh or unreasoning.
He hadn't even been particularly persuasive, at least not in-
tentionally. But Nick remembered how often he had found
himself acquiescing to his father's suggestions, agreeing to
things about which he had vowed to be resolute. He remembered when he had decided to leave the company once
before, to go back to school and study art history with the
idea of going to work for a gallery and someday having one
of his own. Russell had listened patiently, following Nick's
well prepared but clumsily delivered arguments with his
sad, unblinking gaze, while Nick felt the words grow thick
on his tongue and lose the crisp rectitude they'd had in his
mind. Still, he had been prepared for any argument his father might advance except one. Russell sighed, dropped his
eyes to the floor and said, "I understand that, Nick. I once
thought I wanted to be a railroad engineer. But it would
mean an awful lot to me if you'd stay on." That was all,
simple pleading, a request which Nick found he couldn't
refuse. He left his father's house feeling noble, feeling he

had played his part in filial succession, and by the time he got home he was burning with self-disgust and went into a rage at Lesley when she asked him how it had gone.

I'm in my own apartment in New York, and I'm staying, Nick thought. He still wanted his father's approval, but he had Philippa now and a new life on the way to being what he wanted. He paced back to the window in time to look down to the street and see Russell bend to pay the cab driver and then turn and look up at the building as if to fix the place in his mind. His father was wearing a trenchcoat and a slightly battered gray fedora he had had for years. He was one of the few men Nick knew who still wore a hat, and he thought of how much he looked like some quiet Bogart character. Nick turned and scanned the room to see if everything was in order, business papers on the desk suitably spread out as if he had been working, the coffeepot and two cups on the table, Philippa in the next room. He walked to the doorway and watched her check figures from her notes against those on a computer screen.

"He's here," he told her. "Wait till he comes in, then come out and I'll introduce you."

"Would you like me to join you?" she asked.

"No. I don't want to drag it out. I don't want him to start questioning you."

"You're just going to have to stand your ground," she coached.

"I will," he said impatiently, just as the callboard buzzed and filled his stomach with a new wave of queasiness. "Maybe you could come out later," he told her.

"Come on up," he called into the speaker and released the lock on the lobby door three floors below. He walked back to the far side of the room, sat on the edge of a straight-backed chair and waited.

His father looked older and somehow less commanding waiting in the doorway with his hat at his side. I'm not listening, Nick reminded himself. He said hello, took Russell's hat and coat, and motioned toward the living room. He heard Philippa's heels on the hardwood floor and saw her enter the room behind his father. He thought how pretty she looked with her dull blond hair and creamy, pale skin. She was wearing a tailored brown suit with a silk bow tie. He wanted his father to see her as a sensible mature woman, that he hadn't run off with some floozy. He introduced them.

Philippa shook Russell's hand. "I'm happy to meet you."

"I'm pleased to meet you," Russell said. "This is a lovely room."

"Thank you." Philippa smiled sweetly. "It's Nicky's expression as much as mine."

There was an awkward moment of silence, and then Philippa excused herself, informing Russell that she had some work to finish.

"Of course." Russell bowed politely.

"She's preparing some furniture appraisals," Nick explained.

"She's very nice," Russell said. "She has a good grip."

Nick remembered his father's lectures on the importance of a firm handshake. He offered coffee.

"No thanks," Russell said. "I had about ten cups before I came over. I guess I was a little nervous."

Nick was surprised by the admission. They sat facing each other across the coffee table and Russell began talking about the fog and how much colder it had been at home. Nick stiffened at the mention of Five Oaks. He felt they were circling each other defensively, like wrestlers about to engage.

"You seem to be doing well," Russell observed.

"I am. I'm doing better than I can ever remember." Nick wondered if he was sounding too obviously recalcitrant.

"I'm glad to hear that."

"I feel needed here. I feel happier than I've ever been."

"Good." Russell nodded. "You look good."

"I just want to tell you before you get started," Nick gathered himself. "I like what I'm doing here so if you have any arguments about why I should come back to Five Oaks, you can save them."

"No I don't."

"I wanted you to know that. I've never been able to talk to you the way I've wanted to. I never felt you really listened."

"I'm sorry if that's true," Russell said.

"I was always afraid of bothering you."

"Bothering me?"

"You were always so busy. And when I did get to talk to you, I was always afraid you'd get angry."

"Did I get angry a lot?"

"I always thought you did," Nick insisted.

"Well, I think I've changed."

"So have I. I don't care about what you think anymore." Nick winced, wondering if he was sounding a little harsher than he meant to be.

"Oh?" Russell recoiled. "Well, maybe that's good."

"I think it's good," Nick said.

"I can understand that."

"Can you? I don't know if you can."

"I can. I know sometimes you have to make up your mind and not look back."

"That's what it is," Nick insisted. "I'm not looking back. I like what I'm doing. I like where I am. And I feel loved."

"That's important." Russell said. "All those things are important." He looked at Nick and then he looked at the floor. "Nick," he began, "I've changed too. I guess I said that." He shrugged and smiled deferentially. "I've spent a lot of time by myself, and I've been trying to understand a lot of things I hadn't paid much attention to before."

"I've heard."

"You have?"

"Lesley," Nick said.

"We've spent a lot of time together," Russell said. "We both felt pretty empty after you left."

"Is that supposed to make me feel guilty?" Nick asked.

"No, I didn't mean it that way."

"Well, I'm glad you were there." He softened. "I didn't want to leave the way I did. But if I'd talked to her about it, or to you, I wouldn't have been able to do it. It seems like, no matter what it was, no matter what I wanted to do, when I talked to you, I'd end up giving in, and I'd hate myself for it. I felt like a joke, ever since I came back from Viet Nam. I don't blame you. I blame myself. I made myself miserable trying to please you, and I guess I made Lesley miserable too. Nobody wanted to let me do anything because nobody wanted to be responsible if I screwed up. But now I don't care. If I screw up, I'll screw up, but at least I'll know *I* did it."

"That's fair," Russell said. "Maybe I let what I wanted get in the way. Maybe I didn't listen very well."

Nick sat staring at his hands and said nothing.

"But what I wanted to tell you," Russell continued, "is that, as I said, Lesley and I have spent a lot of time together. And Katy," he added. He rubbed his hand over his face as if he were clearing it of cobwebs. "Well, we got to talking and . . ." He stopped himself.

"And?" Nick urged.

"And nothing." Russell shook it off. "It's nothing. I just wanted to tell you that we all still care about you."

"Really?" Nick regarded his father skeptically. "I had the feeling you were going to say something more specific."

"Well I was." Russell rubbed the back of his neck.

"Maybe it's important."

"Maybe," Russell said. "I know you'll find out anyway, sooner or later, so I guess I'd rather have you hear it from me."

"Well?"

Russell nodded and took a deep breath. "Lesley and I have been seeing each other."

"Seeing each other?" Nick's voice was pinched. "You mean like man and woman? Like lovers?"

"Yes."

Nick felt as if he'd misplaced something and was trying to find it in the air around him. "I can't believe it."

"Nick, I . . ."

Nick shook his head. "I mean I just literally can't believe it. You and Lesley?"

"I love her," Russell insisted.

Nick waited for his father to say something further, something to explain that he hadn't really meant what he'd said. They waited for what seemed, to both of them, a very long time.

"We started out consoling each other," Russell said. "And then I discovered I was in love with her."

"I'm stunned," Nick said. "I didn't think you even thought about women anymore."

"Did you think I was too old?"

"Well my God, you're what, thirty years older than she is?"

"Yes. Twenty-nine."

"Well hell, you two always seemed to have something going for each other." Nick rose on the edge of his chair. "I used to get sick of her talking about you. You must have been glad to have me out of the way."

"That's not true. I swear."

"You could've told me you'd decided to marry Josephine or become a Moonie. But my God, Lesley?"

"Nick, I didn't plan it. It just happened."

"What about your precious friends?" Nick insisted. "What about your immaculate reputation?"

"We haven't told anyone," Russell said. "There's this takeover we're fighting."

Nick waited for Russell to say something more, or for something to occur to him. He became aware of the sound of the traffic from the street. He got up from the couch, walked over to the corner of the room and pretended to busy himself with something on his desk. What his father was saying didn't make any sense. It just wasn't possible. "I've got things to do," he said.

"Nick, I'd hoped we could talk about it."

"Talk about it?" Nick screamed. "What's to talk about? You got what you wanted."

"I got what you didn't want." Russell stood up. "I got what you walked out on. You've been doing that all your life, turning your back on anything that was the least bit tough to handle."

Nick made some scribbles on a notepad. "Was there anything else?" He spoke without looking up.

"Nick, I'm sorry. I didn't mean that. I don't want it to be this way. I just wanted to . . ."

"Get it off your chest?" Nick suggested. "I think you wanted one last shot at telling me how right you are, how right you've always been. You're a lot like Lesley that way, always some final words of wisdom. I used to wonder how much time the two of you spent talking about me, as if I were some disease you shared. Maybe you wanted her all along. Well, now you can have her because I just don't give a fuck."

"Nick," Russell sighed heavily. "I swear I didn't have any designs on Lesley. I've always loved her as a daughter. What happened just happened. You were gone, and we needed each other. We both loved you. We both still do. You're still part of the family. Katy's still your daughter. We're not shutting you out."

"It's a little late for that." Nick laughed sardonically. "I haven't been part of your family. I don't even think there ever was a family. Philippa's my family." He could feel himself trembling. He wanted his father to leave and take his stifling reality with him.

"Nick, I'm sorry. I'd hoped . . ."

"I know what you hoped." Nick cut him off. "You hoped I'd say, 'Gee, that's great Dad.' Well, I won't. I think it stinks. I want you to know that. I want you to live with it." The light from the desk lamp blurred his view of his father's face.

"I don't know what I'd hoped." Russell sounded deflated, but calm. "I guess I wanted to tell you that I love you."

Nick snorted. He turned his back and looked out the window, looking down at the rain on Columbus Avenue. A man on the far sidewalk held an opened newspaper above his head as a makeshift umbrella, in what seemed a posture of surrender. "Don't forget your coat," he said.

ON HIS WAY BACK ACROSS the park, Russell didn't notice anything beyond the dirty ashtray smell of the cab and the plastic sign thanking passengers for not smoking. He closed his eyes and dissolved into the thudding and rumbling of the taxi. How could I have been so stupid? How could I have expected Nick to understand what I don't understand? He felt bile in his throat, and wished he could simply cease to exist, become a tree or a park bench, anything free of emotion or thought. He wondered if he might have made a better life for all of them if he had spent more time simply enjoying his, and less energy trying to make something out of it.

He had booked tickets for the theater that evening, but when he told Lesley what had happened with Nick, she understood why he didn't want to go. Russell arranged for the Lear to meet them in White Plains and called the hotel desk to say they would be checking out earlier than planned.

In the elevator on their way down to the lobby, the bellman told Russell that they had missed his regular visits and that his stay this time had been too brief.

"Yes it has," Russell agreed and thanked him. He made an excuse about the press of business and said that he hoped to come back soon. The bellman said he would take the bags to the limousine and meet them by the front door.

The cashier seemed to be much too young, a gangly schoolboy dressed up in a morning coat and striped trousers. Russell signed his American Express slip, folded his itemized bill and slid it into his inside coat pocket. He turned from the desk to look for Lesley, and the bellman was there with his practiced smile.

"Your bags are all loaded, Mr. Wheeler," he said. He took the folded money Russell handed him. "Thank you very much sir," he said. "Your daughter has already gone out to the car."

37

A WEEK LATER, UNDER A NEARLY full moon, the Lear climbed towards 40,000 feet and the lights of Chicago splayed out in an almost perfect grid. Russell thought of photographs of microscopically illuminated snowflakes he had seen in a recent *Smithsonian*. He couldn't remember the air ever being so clear. He fixed himself a bourbon and water and looked down on the city, as if it had been electrified purely for his delight. He was relieved to have his deposition behind him. The lawyers for United Tobacco had tried to make an issue of the Wheeler Stock he had sold at thirty-two dollars a share from his Uncle Wallace's estate three years earlier. They asked how he could justify his having sold at that price with his refusal of their offer of sixty. Russell explained that as sole trustee of the estate, he hadn't chosen to sell at thirty-two, but that the Internal Revenue Service had demanded payment of the estate taxes and that he'd had no choice but to sell enough stock to cover it. He elicited a stage laugh from his attorneys when he had told United's counsel that he had offered the IRS his marker, but that they had insisted on cash.

The light show faded behind them as they reached the shore and headed over the moonlit gulf of Lake Michigan. He had planned to spend the night in Chicago, anticipating further depositions in the morning, but the opposing attorneys had tired of him when they found his testimony wasn't helping them establish their offer as a fair one and the antitrust suit as merely a diversion to protect the present management of the company. The jet had brought over some company research personnel who were to be deposed the next day, and Russell decided to catch a ride home with the pilots.

That morning at the Ritz–Carlton, he had received a call from Tom Carey. Their attorneys in Richmond had uncovered a payment of almost two-and-a-half million dollars United had made to officials of the Canadian government to ignore import tarriffs that would have cost United nearly ten million.

"It may be just the break we've been looking for," Tom said gleefully. "They may decide we're not worth having that brought out in court and possibly triggering an investigation."

Another drink deepened the satisfaction Russell felt over how well things seemed to be working out. Tom had also told him that he and Lesley had had a wonderful time at the Muscular Dystrophy Society Ball the previous evening. He mentioned how thoroughly she seemed to have rebounded and how gay, almost ecstatic, she had been. Russell couldn't help thinking that Tom must have misinterpreted the source of her joy.

He could hear Lily's frantic yowling as he fumbled with his keys, a kind of scolding, whining chirp as if admonishing him for having left her. Even when he had only been away overnight she performed a canine *Camille*, to impress him with the anxiety he had caused her and to ensure he would assuage it with a Milkbone. He had called Josephine from Chicago to let her know of his early return, and she had left a small casserole of sausage, cheese, tomato and fettuccine on the counter for him to microwave. She'd also left on a few lights to cheer his return, including those strung in the bare flowering crab in the front yard and the strings of red pin-lights in the artificial holly. These reminded him that it was only three days until Christmas, and it occurred to him that after his supper, while Katy was sleeping, might be an ideal time to deliver the enormous plush tiger he had bought for her in New York.

The tiger filled the cargo area of his Blazer, its silver dollar-sized eyes peering over his shoulder. It reminded him of an old movie in which Laurel and Hardy are oblivious to the live lion in the back seat of their Model T. If his stock-holders could see him now, they might feel relieved he had retired.

Without the cover of clouds to contain it, what modest warmth the earth had absorbed during its brief exposure to the winter sun had been drawn off by the stars, or so Russell liked to think; stars like sirens, singing in the cold. At times, on clear nights like this, he stood out on the ice cover of the lake and imagined he felt them pulling him, gravity dissipating under his feet. Where the road dipped along the edge of the marsh, the frosted trees and the pods of the cattails glittered in his highbeams. He was full of yuletide frivolity as he negotiated Lesley's meandering driveway, anxious to tell her the news about United's illegal kickbacks, to show her the tiger and to hear her account of the ball. He was also more than a little pleased by the prospect of Katy's being in bed and of their having what was left of the evening to themselves. He had broken into the opening bars of "Got A Date With An Angel" when his headlights picked up the familiar shape of Tom Carey's BMW in front of her garage, and the singing stopped.

Russell switched off his headlights and sat listening to his engine idle in the darkness, wondering what Tom's car was doing there and what he ought to do about it. There were lights on inside the house but no one had come to the windows. He tried to imagine what might happen if he rang the doorbell. It was 10:15 by his watch. They might only be talking, but talking about what? Tom's hopes might have been inflated by their evening at the ball. If he had stopped by unannounced, Lesley would, of course, have to be gracious. She couldn't very well turn him away for the sake of a propriety he couldn't know about. Nothing could happen with Katy there, anyway.

But why? Russell kept his headlights off until he had retreated round the bend of the driveway and the house was blocked by the trees. He would come back later and pretend he hadn't seen Tom's car, pretend he had only just returned from Chicago; he would play dumb until Lesley told him all about it.

He drove into Five Oaks and, despite a nagging anxiety, enjoyed the nearly deserted streets and the Christmas lights of the houses closed up against the cold. He remembered having spent time at Christmas in some of these houses as a child, houses that had belonged to friends of his parents or his grandparents and which had since been bought and restored by Wheeler executives who had perhaps sold them in turn to other executives when they had been transferred or left the company. He liked to imagine his father and his grandfather walking those streets in an earlier time, and even his martyred great-grandfather, whose life must have had some moments of peace, though none had been chronicled.

He turned around and drove back up Main, but this time he felt the emptiness of the sidewalks. Even the bars appeared abandoned to the winter night. Now that emptiness made him feel old, and he recalled a discussion he'd had with Lesley just a week earlier about their old friend, Thoreau. It had been triggered by his observation that Thoreau seemed to have been an antifeminist.

"Of course I've heard that before," Lesley had replied, and asked what, specifically, he was referring to.

"Well, he says that what's chiefly required in any argument with a woman is courtesy. That you have to fire blanks rather than giving them your full shot."

"I think he was criticizing the dilemma of some women as they saw themselves at that time, wanting to argue on equal footing with a man and yet be paid the deference due a lady." Russell sensed a certain edge to her voice.

"I have to confess that I'm old fashioned enough to like that idea."

"But it's having your cake and eating it too."

"My mother always used to say that, and it's never made sense to me. What's the point of having your cake if you can't eat it? Who wants to collect a lot of stale cake?"

"I think it's a statement about greed," Lesley countered.

"But what he's getting at is that if women want to be on equal footing with men, they have to come out from behind the protection of being women."

"Well, I don't see what's so great about being equal with a man. And I don't mean equal rights. It seems a kind of diminishment to me."

"That's a noble, outmoded old attitude. It keeps women in their place by keeping them on a pedestal."

"Maybe I'm a noble, outmoded old person," he said.

"In some ways you are," she concluded. It was the first time she had shown him any hardness in all the years he had known her.

IT WAS MIDNIGHT WHEN HE again turned into Lesley's drive. He switched off his lights and navigated solely by the light of the moon and the snow. A white night, he thought, rationalizing his stealth as a way of appreciating the beauty of the moonlight rather than as an exercise in deception. What is there to be deceptive about? He cleared the trees at the bend and caught his first glimpse of the house.

From the light over the garage, he could see that Tom's car was gone. But how long had it been there? What time had he arrived? Russell could see that the lights inside the house had been turned off. It's too late now, he thought. I couldn't pretend I didn't know. He saw Lesley in her black dress at the Christmas party, blushing as Tom bent close. He couldn't recall her blushing that way with him. He saw her again in postures he had just come to know, her beautiful legs raised and bent back, her face flushed, her mouth open in a cry of pleasure. Three quarters of a tank, the sound of his own breathing; he was staring at the fuel guage, and it was three-fourths full.

He drove home very slowly, looking out over the moon-covered land, wondering what it was that had made it so beautiful before.

38

Twelve days after the work on the airstrip had begun, Kopa ki used his machete to chop off the little finger of his left hand at the first joint. It was a sacrifice to the spirit of his first wife, Neggi, the mother of Matu, who was dying of the laughing death, which the People called kuru. The day after the plane had dropped its supplies and instructions for the strip, a creeping paralysis had set in, beginning in the muscles of Neggi's legs and moving up to her throat, until she could no longer swallow. In her last hours, she was racked with fits of uncontrollable laughter, her eyes blank and shining as if life had already left them and her body had been abandoned to the cachinating demon she had become. Russell had seen this kind of death before among the People and knew there was nothing to be done. He sat with Neggi all night and poured water over her face and breast to cool her fever, while Kopa ki crouched outside with his hands over his ears, trying to keep out the sound of her horrible cackling. He refused to be in the hut with her because he was afraid she might try to take him with her when she died. Several times Russell tried to pour a little water into Neggi's mouth, but it only caused her laughing to become more violent and grotesque as the water gushed back out in a white froth.

When the sun broke over the eastern mountains and the first light through the window cast Russell's shadow across her, Neggi stopped laughing as abruptly as a radio being turned off, and her body stiffened as if rigor mortis itself had been the cause of death. Russell was exhausted and sat staring at her in the startling silence until he saw Kopa ki's shadow rise above the threshold behind him.

"She has gone, Quari?"

"Yes." Russell nodded. "I was afraid she would want me to be her husband in the Land of the Dead. She was jealous of Kantu."

"Maybe she has found a husband," Russell said absently.

"Maybe so, Quari. Maybe my father or my brother who was taken by the People Born of Pigs."

Neggi's body was taken to the the mortuary pit where the beetles would clean it to the bone, so that Matu could sleep with her skull and so placate her spirit. Russell and Kopa ki were returning to Tapua when they heard the plane thunder over the covering trees, followed by the thrashing wings of a dozen startled hornbills. They exchanged a quick glance and sprinted toward the village. Russell was out of breath when they reached the clearing. He could see the tribesmen already sliding and scrambling down the slope toward the valley floor.

"He has come Quari." Kopa ki reached up and took Russell's hand.

"Yes," Russell gasped, and they were off again running, skidding down the trail to the airstrip.

The villagers had been rallied by the elders around the conical orange flag they had been told would coax the Great Bird down from the sky. They broke into spontaneous songs of praise to the miraculous machetes with which they had chopped the grass to its roots. How easily they would use them to chop down the People Born of Pigs when next they met to exchange insults.

The plane had circled twice and was on its final approach when Russell noticed several of the newly initiated men standing on the runway with their arms outstretched to the descending god. He yelled to Kopa ki and together they chased the fledgling warriors off the field, but not before the plane had to pull up for another go-round. On its second approach, the People chanted a song they normally sang to welcome the God of Vegetable Growth to their garden plots, and as the plane touched down, they uttered the collective "Ahh," of satisfaction Russell had heard when a successful hunting party returned to the village.

The plane bounced and took flight twice before it settled, turned and began its bumpy taxi to where they were assembled.

Russell shouted, trying to keep the People back from the plane, but his voice was lost in the excitement, and they were already crowding in around it, chanting and bowing rhythmically. The engine noise died, and as abruptly as the propellor stopped, the People grew silent. There was a sharp explosion, and they scattered. The fuselage rocked, and Russell saw a huge, red-faced man dressed in khaki and a navy baseball cap standing next to the wing. He was brandishing an automatic pistol and shouting in a language the severity and precision of which Russell had all but forgotten.

"Tell those Abos to stay clear of my plane." The tribesmen stopped running, turned and knelt facing the pilot. "You there," the pilot pointed toward Russell and then beckoned with his gun hand, "come on over here." Russell recognized the accent as Australian.

"You really a white man? Whee! Couldn't prove it by me. Auken's the name." He extended his hand and Russell took it. He had forgotten how large a man's hand could be.

"Wheeler," he said. The name felt alien to him, as if he were repeating a word he had only just learned.

"A Yank!" Auken smiled. "I knew you'd be a Yank. How long you been here?"

The People moved closer and stood listening with respect to this strange talk of the sky people. "I don't know," Russell said.

"Oh, a long time then." Auken chuckled. "You look like you been here a good long time."

Seeing Auken dressed and clean-shaven made Russell aware of the length of his beard and his hair and of his own nakedness. "What year is it?" he asked.

"What year is it?" Auken bellowed. "What year is it, man? What year is it you got lost? If you remember."

"1942. December, I think."

"Keerikey! Well, you've been here exactly three years then." Auken cocked his head as if in amazement. "It's the day after Christmas 1945." He turned and rummaged around in the plane and came back with a rumpled pair of khaki shorts in his hand. "Here, Adam," he said, handing them to Russell, "welcome back to the civilized world."

The People, who had been silent, began a low talking among themselves. They inched back in around the plane, and Russell heard Kopa ki's voice close behind him. "Quari," he asked, "is this your father?"

"What's that?" Auken inquired.

"My friend," Russell told him, "the man who rescued me when my plane crashed. He wants to know if you are the God of the Sky. I told them you were the God of the Sky."

"Sure," Auken said, "I can be that. I can be jolly old Saint Nick or the Queen of the May. Are there any more of you here?"

"Any more?"

"Yanks. White men?"

"No," Russell said, "only me."

"We plotted at least three planes down in this region, but so far you're the only survivor we've found. Just bloody luck I spotted your hide." Auken took a blue bandana from his hip pocket. He lifted his baseball cap and wiped his forehead. "I don't want to rush your farewell here, but we've got a long flight, and I want to make it while we've got daylight." He stuffed the bandana back in his pocket and looked at the spears and the wildly painted faces around them. "Christ, I've never seen woolier looking Abos than these. I'm surprised they didn't eat you."

Russell turned to Kopa ki. "No," he said, "this is not the God of the Sky. This is only his messenger. He has come to take me home."

"Will you take me with you?" Kopa ki asked it as a child would ask. "I would like to meet your father."

"What's he saying?" Auken asked.

"He wants to come with us."

"Christ! That's all I need, flying man-eaters to Port Moresby."

"But he's . . ." Russell started to explain to Auken, then turned back to Kopa ki. "No," he said, "I must go alone this time. But I will come back for you with much magic."

"No, Quari, please." Kopa ki was pleading. "I'm afraid I will never see you again." He grasped Russell's hand.

"You would not like it where I am going. The beings who live there would put you in a cage. They would treat you like an opossum. But I will come back to Tapua with many gifts."

The talk among the People was louder now, more animated, and they were edging closer to the plane.

"Look, mate, I don't like this," Auken said. "I suggest you get yourself in on board and tell your fuzzy-wuzzy to back off."

"It's okay," Russell assured Auken, "this is my friend."

Auken smiled sardonically. "Like a pet viper's your friend." He shook his head. "Look Yank, I didn't come here to export no Guinea men. I been lookin' for a plane that went down a month ago, and it's just blind luck I spotted you. Now I hung my ass out to get your outta here, so I suggest you strap yourself in cause its gonna be a bit rough."

Russell looked at Kopa ki and saw the sad face of a child, a bizarre child with feathers in his hair and a ring of bone in his nose. But he was thinking only of Port Moresby and the distant place he remembered as home. "No." Russell tried to sound stern. "I must go alone."

"Please Quari! I have never had a friend like you."

"No!" Russell barked. He shook his hand free of Kopa ki's grasp. Once more he told Kopa ki that he would come back for him, but this time he was looking at the mountains beyond Kopa ki's head, and his face burned with the lie as he spoke it. He turned away abruptly, opened the door of the plane and climbed into the copilot's seat. He busied himself adjusting the seat belt and avoided the face that watched him. Auken climbed in the other door, fastened his seat belt and shouted, "Clear!"

The starter whined and the propeller made two laborious rotations. Then the radial engine gave off a puff of gray smoke as it coughed and exploded into life. Russell concentrated on the panel before him. It all looked so strange, the flat metal surfaces, the precise circular gauges, the lights, the switches, the printed words, "tab, trim, flap and rudder," the rhythmical vibration, the smell of gasoline. Through the ordeal of Neggi's death, he had all but forgotten about the plane, and now it was all he cared about. One minute he had been consoling Kopa ki as a friend, and the next, scolding him as one scolds a child and making promises he knew he would never keep. He pretended to be studying the gauges though it was Kopa ki's eyes he saw in the panel before him. He felt himself rocked as the plane began taxiing.

"You didn't do a half-bad job here," Auken shouted. "These Abos could make fair Sea Bees. I've flown strips worse than this."

Russell glanced out the window. The other tribesmen were standing under the windsock, but Kopa ki wasn't among them. Auken kicked the rudder and spun the plane into position for takeoff.

"What about the war?" Russell shouted.

"What's that?" Auken was running up the engine to check the magneto.

"The war? Did we ever take Buna?"

"Oh Christ man," Auken hollered. "That's all done. We drove the Japs back to Yokohama. And you Yanks dropped one huge bomb on 'em."

"One bomb?" Russell was sure he hadn't heard correctly.

"Well two, actually," Auken said. "Christ man, the world's changed. Wait till you get to Port Moresby. You've got some catching up to do. You can take a bath too. Keerikey, do you stink!"

Auken pushed in the throttle. The engine strained a moment, and they began moving forward. "Christ, this is sticky." Auken muttered. They picked up speed and the bouncing became more regular. Russell watched the stick jostle in Auken's hand. He glanced out at the People as the plane hurtled past them. They were pointing and gesturing wildly.

"Here we go." Auken pulled back the stick. The plane took one last great bounce into the air, and Russell felt his stomach drop. Then suddenly the plane lurched, the right wing dipping sharply toward the ground.

"Christ!" Auken pulled the stick toward him, fighting it. The plane shuddered and banked. "Something's tits up here!" he screamed.

Russell twisted in his seat and looked out the window. At first glance he saw only the tribesmen below who were scattering wildly like a frightened herd. And when he did see it, he couldn't speak. Auken was cursing as he struggled for control of the stick. Russell pulled the latch cord and tried to push the door open, but the wind pressure forced it back on him.

"What the fuck?" Auken yelled.

Russell managed to work his hand through the opening, managed to clutch the other hand with its mutilated finger on the wing-strut before it was torn from his grasp, and for an instant he looked into the fierce expression of Kopa ki's eyes superimposed against the valley floor. His mouth was open to the word Russell heard as a scream in his own throat as the savage face was swept from him.

"What the fuck was that?" Auken demanded.

"Quari," Russell mouthed the word, numbly.

"What?" Auken shrieked.

"Quari," Russell repeated as if to himself. "It means friend."

The plane, now free of its encumbrance, leveled and climbed through the dense clear air toward the rim of the nameless green mountains.

39

THE SUMMER EVERYONE WAS SINGING "Volare," Russell and Miriam arrived in Brussels for the World's Fair. A policeman sang it in front of their hotel, and they heard it again outside the Russian Pavillion where they viewed a replica of Sputnik, watched over by matrons in sensible oxfords. They heard it in London, in Paris and, of course, in Rome. He remembered an afternoon spent in their room at the Excelsior following a leisurely lunch, feeling the warmth of the sunlight which came through the curtains with the muffled cacophony of the Via Veneto. He angled a mirrored door of the armoire at the foot of their bed so they could watch themselves, and they made love to completion more than once, the only time they'd done that since their first year together. Miriam kissed the birthmark on his shoulder and called him her "moonman" again. And afterwards they went down to a sidewalk cafe, still rank from their lovemaking. They sat and sipped Campari and soda and felt both earthy and exalted.

And Russell recalled something else long-forgotten, an afternoon on the forecastle of the troop ship, steaming homeward in mid-Pacific, when a group of soldiers, mostly replacements who had come out after his plane had been lost, sat together reverently as if giving testimony in church and tried to recall or imagine the smell of a woman. Like fish, one thought, but not like fish, like honey, like the smell of dew or like warm bread, just slightly yeasty, like rain in the air after a long dry spell or cinnamon or sour apples or simply like the perfume they had chosen. One boy, whom Russell felt certain could not have yet turned eighteen, described the way his mother smelled when she had rocked him in her arms the night before he had left home, the smell of her powder and the elastic of her bra, and no one had laughed at him. There was no effort to impress or to ridicule, and each man had told what he knew as if talking of a landscape he had once loved and hoped he might find again, though he would no longer be the boy who had loved it.

40

JANUARY 4TH. WHY DID THIS DATE seem significant? It occurred to him that as he got older almost every day had become an anniversary of some kind, the birth date or death date of someone he had loved. It would be nice, he thought, to selectively cull his memories the way he might discard old letters from his files or books he knew he wouldn't read again from his shelves.

After lunch, Russell laced up his Sorels and headed out for the mailbox with Lily trotting along behind him. Powdery new snow splayed out before him with each step, bow waves from a skiff in rough water. He recalled that Eskimos were said to distinguish forty kinds of snow and wondered which of those forty this might be. For some reason, Neil Hazzard hadn't plowed the drive. Russell made a mental note to call him about it when he got back to the house. It was the second time this winter the drive hadn't been cleared before noon. The uniform whiteness was broken by a border of fenceposts, power poles stretching across the field, the hulking shape of a barn and the dark silhouette of the woods across the road. How different winter must be on the prairie, he thought, a sea of rolling snow blending almost imperceptibly into the pale gray sky. There were several places along his cross-country ski trails where he could look up the slope of a bare hill to the nothing above it and imagine he was in Nebraska or South Dakota or in some polar region where no structure of life invaded the horizon. *A blanker whiteness of benighted snow.* He called up the line from a poem he had read to Lesley.

Over Christmas, she had made no mention of having

seen Tom Carey other than on their evening at the ball, which she simply described as "great fun." And he discovered that the evening he had returned from Chicago to find Tom's car in her drive, Katy had spent the night at the home of a friend.

The next day, he had returned to deliver the tiger and found no one at home. He let himself in the back door and carried the tiger to Lesley's study, a spare bedroom she had set up as her office and which became, for the Christmas season, her wrapping room. Katy knew this room was off limits, and the tiger would be safe here from her prying eyes. He went to Lesley's desk to leave her a note explaining the tiger's presence, but when he opened a folder, looking for a scrap of paper, he found a note already there, a draft of a note in Lesley's hand.

> Dear Tom, I wasn't quite honest with you last night when I told you it was too soon. It's not too soon. My relationship with Nick has been over for years. I would like to see more of you, to know who you are. I want to—I really do. It's just that this whole break-up business has been pretty hard on Russell, and I don't want to cause him any further upset right now. He's been so good to me, so kind, so much more a father than any father I've known. He has to be my priority right now. I would hate, more than anything, to cause him any more distress. So please understand. I only hope you have patience, that in waiting for time to do its work, you will still want to pursue this.
> Fondly, Lesley

KATY WAS THRILLED WITH the stuffed tiger, which stood exactly to her height. In the Polaroid photograph he took of her standing beside it Christmas morning, their eyes lined up as straight as the stars in the belt of Orion. And Lesley seemed pleased with the diamond pin he had bought for her in Grand Rapids when he had gone for his physical with Warren Riordan. But he sensed ambivalence in her gratitude.

The fragrance of the gardenia corsage Tom had bought Lesley for the ball lingered about her house for several days. It was ironic to Russell that the scent which most evoked her presence for him now was that of a gift from Tom. He could feel what he wanted to say to her. He could see it almost as a geometric shape, but he couldn't find words for it, couldn't alter the disparity in their ages or turn her deeply felt gratitude to love. He accepted the affection she granted him as he gratefully accepted each breath as it came to him, breaths that seemed to come harder now. But still, he wanted to possess her one more time, always once more, to see her head thrown back on the pillow, urging him more deeply into her. He wanted to hear those cries from her throat, to know he was pleasing her—he had kept a respectable distance so long—to look up the plane of her belly, to taste her, knowing it was her and no one else, to see the diamond stud in her earlobe, her auburn hair on the pillow. Each time he worried that it might be the last, and that itself was a kind of death.

Lesley's present to Russell had been a large glazed porcelain egg she had found in a shop on Madison the day he had gone to see Nick. It was hand-lettered in French with what he supposed was meant to have been an endearing inscription. She had translated it as *Men are more like melons, the more mature, the better.*

He reflected that the connotation of the message may have changed since the day she purchased it. On Christmas morning, it had struck him as somewhat patronizing. She might very well continue her charade out of long-standing gratitude, he thought. He imagined her caring for him in his dotage, changing his bedpan before slipping off to her rendezvous with Tom.

When he was with her, life itself seemed reason enough to continue. Other times, it was only something to do, something that wasn't very interesting anymore. When they had been purely soul mates, he hadn't thought of losing her. Now he thought of little else. Where there had been comfort, there was now only apprehension. Her attentiveness had begun to feel like ritual. He sensed her distraction, and when he looked at her now, he saw the space she occupied as a potential void. Christmas night he suggested they make love, though he hadn't been at all sure he would be able. And Lesley had declined, claiming to be tired. He wanted to tell her what he knew about the note, but that would change everything. She would lie to protect his feelings. Or else she might tell him the truth. And he didn't want to hear that either.

He looked out over the pasture, not a mark of a weed or of any stubble showing through, a near-perfect blankness sculpted by the wind. When he came to the end of his drive, he discovered that the road hadn't been plowed either, and he saw the lone tracks of Charlie Willis's Bronco angling under his mailbox in the otherwise untroubled snow.

With Christmas past, the flood of catalogues had subsided. There were only a few announcing January white sales, along with a smattering of charitable solicitations, a handful of bills, and the familiar chrome yellow of *National Geographic*. The mail was nearly always a disappointment to Russell. He didn't know what he ever expected it to bring him, and apart from a rare personal letter, satisfaction never came. He glanced at the cover of the magazine and spotted an article titled "The Stone Age Still Lives in New Guinea" between "A New England Village Reclaims Its Heritage," and "Faulkner's Mississippi Revisited." He smiled at this. He'd read dozens of stories about yet another primitive enclave which had theretofore been spared dissection by cultural anthropologists. It amused him to compare their discoveries with his memories of the People. He folded the bundle, tucked it under his arm, and retraced his footprints back toward the house.

He noticed how his shoulders were hunched against the cold, how he felt it in his bones. This winter he was having more trouble adjusting to it. He had a theory that as the body grew older it generated less heat, like a battery losing its charge or a fire dying out as its fuel dwindled. He doubted it had any scientific validity, but he felt it was true.

Maybe it accounted for the gray pallor about old people, gray faces, gray lips, gray hair. Maybe they were just very gradually going cold. He tried to relax his shoulders. He walked faster, and he noticed how much harder his breath came.

After he sorted the form letters, the catalogues and the bills, he poured himself another cup of coffee and sat down to discover what had been rediscovered this time in New Guinea. He read of a village encountered by a team from the U.S. Army's Central Identification Laboratory, isolated in a crater high in the Sepic River region of the Owen Stanley Range. A village called Tapua. Russell closed the magazine on his thumb and took a moment to catch his breath. Did he really want to read this one? He wondered if it might not be better to leave Tapua as he had known it, not to rile himself with the invasion of a private memory, a private dream. He sat for a moment and looked out over the frozen lake, the white nothing he wanted this story to be.

It began with an explanation of the Central Identification Labratory, or CIL, and its mission, which was to locate and identify the remains of all the flyers unaccounted for in the over three hundred and fifty U.S. planes lost in the Owen Stanleys during War II. The article went on to discuss the geography of the region, the fact that no roads of any kind connected the major cities, and to explain how it would be possible, after all these years, for this village, with its unique and anachronistic language, to have remained almost totally innocent of the twentieth century. The CIL team had found one man in the village with light brown skin and one blue eye, the result, they assumed, of a marriage with another tribe, some members of which must have, at some point, interbred with whites. They had also found several manufactured items, most likely acquired through conquest or trade with other tribes, or salvaged from one of the downed planes for which the team had been searching. These included several machetes of Australian manufacture, a badly rusted U.S. Army M1 rifle, and a green beer bottle which had become an icon of the tribe and was housed, along with the skull of a former chief, in a little thatched shrine adorned with a carving of a cresent moon on a hillside above the spirit house. The village headman, a man of indeterminate age named Matu, told the legend of his people having been visited by a god from the sky. According to his story, given in a language from which the authors could make only the most rudimentary translation, the god had come down to his people bearing the moon on his shoulder. He had lived with them for a time and had then ascended again to the heavens, taking with him the spirit of their chief and leaving the green bottle as his promise to one day return and to bring them all the gifts of the stars. The authors classified this story under the rubric of "cargo cult beliefs," common to many primitive people who had been exposed to modern artifacts, the origin of which they couldn't explain.

Though like most of the seven hundred tribes in New Guinea, the people of Tapua had once practiced cannibalism, they no longer did. Matu, the headman, said they had given it up as the result of a divine decree—their visitor from the heavens had told them they must no longer eat their enemies. The authors theorized the more likely reason to be that all the neighboring tribes with which they had once warred and upon which they had feasted had been civilized and at least partially absorbed into the national economy.

The same future, the authors suggested, awaited the people of Tapua. Malnutrition had been found throughout the tribe, due largely to the depletion of the available soil for growing the sweet potatos and taro which were their staple diet. New Guinea was geologically so young and its soil so easily exhausted that, year by year, the garden plots which supported the life of the village had had to be planted farther and farther away, and, as Tapua had no chemicals with which to replenish those taken from its soil, it would, if left to its own devices, face extinction within a decade.

The authors concluded sadly that in time either the government or private companies would step in and evacuate the villagers to Port Moresby or Nadzub or Dobodura to work as "cargo boys," unskilled laborers on government road projects, or as sap carriers on rubber plantations where their greatest ambition might be to one day become the driver of a produce truck.

Russell closed the magazine and sat staring at the face of the New England Yankee on the cover. Why should it matter, he wondered. Why should he care about a crude, ignorant people as far away from where he lived as it was possible to get on earth? If the United Tobacco Company had its way, the people of Five Oaks could face extinction themselves. Not extinction perhaps, but dislocation and a complete disruption of their lives.

Maybe it was that men who knew the world could somehow help themselves, or so he believed. Men like himself would always find ways to get along, to thrive. Most of them would. But the People still lived in earth's childhood, unaware that the garden had been invaded by the aphids of what the white men called progress, and that they themselves were now merely a collection of relics to be studied and then sold off.

Russell walked to his den and poured himself a fairly large glass of bourbon. He held the glass up and contemplated the dark amber liquid in the gray winter light from the window. He took a long swallow and felt the bite of it in his throat and the almost immediate warming of his brain. Maybe that's the answer, he thought. Oblivion. He thought of how trivial his own desires seemed, as if viewed again from the window of the plane at forty-thousand feet.

41

Russell shivered in the chill of the examination room. He got up, lifted his shirt from the hook on the wall where it covered his sportcoat, draped it over his shoulders and returned to his perch on the examining table. Warren Riorden had been probing Russell's chest with his frigid stethoscope when he had been called away by the nurse, who had drawn blood from Russell upon his arrival. Russell smiled to himself. Sitting there half-naked, he felt like so much prime beef hung in a cooler to age. He concocted a few remarks for Warren's return about economizing on heat at the expense of patient comfort. Maybe that's why they call us patients, he mused.

Warren had called Russell that morning to ask if he would mind coming down to his office. "A couple of tests we want to run again," he had said. "Probably a mix-up in the lab. The more automated these procedures become the less proficient the technicians seem to be." Russell had come in the week before for his annual physical, and had been pleased to have the ordeal behind him. He always enjoyed his visits with Warren, the reminiscences and stories of hunting and fishing they inevitably shared as they reviewed his medical history. But the idea of needles and the discomfort and medieval indignity of the proctoscope always induced an anticipatory dread verging on nausea.

Russell scanned the framed photographs which nearly covered the wall before him and found among them several taken on their hunting trips to South Dakota: he and Boy and Art and Warren kneeling by the old De Soto, a dozen pheasants lined up on the ground before them. There was a

picture of a dinner party in the front yard of Boy's farmhouse, all the hunters and Boy's family seated around the
harvest table Russell and his friends had presented to the
household in appreciation of Boy's and Myrna's hospitality.
It reminded Russell of historic photos he had seen of early
settlers on the plains, replicating scenes from the darkness
of their sod huts in the photogenic light of day. Jugs, fruit-
jars and pheasant carcasses covered the table and the revelers
were all turned toward the camera, squinting and shading
their eyes from the sun.

There was another photo that caught Russell's eye, and
he bent forward to inspect it more closely. It showed him
and Boy on the rickety kitchen steps behind Boy's house,
plucking the pheasants they had shot that day. The picture
was taken the day Boy first noticed the birthmark on Russell's shoulder and told him it signified some special destiny,
that such a perfect crescent wouldn't appear without purpose. It had been an unusually hot afternoon and he and Boy
had stripped to the waist before beginning work.

"In the old days," Boy said, "that would've marked you
as a medicine man or a potential chief."

Russell asked what the difference was between them.

"A medicine man is someone who has a vision and has to
follow his own particular path, no matter what people
think. And often they think he's crazy."

Breast feathers clung to the blood on Russell's fingers as
he plucked. When he tried to pull them off one hand, they
stuck to the other.

"Maybe he is crazy." Boy continued grinning. "People
thought Jesus was crazy too. But all the wisdom of our
people came from men who were crazy like that."

"So Jesus was a medicine man?" Russell asked. A feather
floated up and clung to his nose. He extended his lower lip
and tried to blow it away.

"I think he was a chief too," Boy said. "Every real man
is a chief." He laughed at Russell and brushed the feather
from his nose. "His people see that in him," he went on. "A
medicine man's someone who cares more about his people

than he does about what he wants for himself. But to him there's no difference. He's just an ordinary man who knows that when he's taking care of his people, he takes care of himself too." Boy rinsed the plucked carcass in the pan of water on the steps between them. "That's like you, I think, Russ." He shook the water off his hand and reached down for another bird. "A chief lives for his people, and he will die for them too, if it's what he should do. He'll get out of the way when his time is through, like Crazy Horse. Crazy Horse knew that if he let the soldiers put him in jail at Fort Robinson, it would break the spirit of his people. He knew he couldn't win. He probably knew his people were finished, but he couldn't let their spirit be destroyed. So he fought the soldiers and they killed him."

"Who am I supposed to fight?" Russell asked.

"Nobody, I guess," Boy said. "I just like to talk about Crazy Horse."

Russell examined the photograph again and saw something in it he had never noticed before. He discerned the silhouette of a woman; Myrna's silhouette it must have been, framed in the screen door behind them.

When Warren returned, Russell quipped about the chill of the examining room. "Don't you pay your heating bills?" he asked.

"Sorry, Russ." Warren smiled, then shook his head. "You gave me a scare these last couple of days."

"A scare?" Russell laughed nervously.

"Go ahead and get dressed." Warren nodded towards Russell's clothes. "My darkest nightmare." Warren placed his hand on Russell's shoulder. "I was afraid I was going to have to give you the worst kind of news. There was some confusion at the lab, and it looked as if your blood work had come back positive for granulocytic leukemia."

"But it didn't?" Russell straightened up and studied Warren's face.

"No, thank God. I think I might sue the lab for causing extreme mental anguish. They had your results mixed up with those of another patient."

"Who?" Russell blurted out. "I'm sorry. That's not my business."

"I understand." Warren peered over the rim of his glasses. "You wonder who's going in your place."

Russell nodded.

"Unfortunately, it's a sixteen-year-old girl. I have to deal with that this afternoon. Don't misunderstand me Russ, but it would have been less difficult news to break if it had been you, or myself for that matter. But I'm glad it's not you."

"I understand." Russell buttoned his shirt. "Sixteen years old, Jesus! What does it mean, granulocytic leukemia?"

"It means her blood cells are at war with each other."

"Is there any hope?"

Warren shook his head.

"What will it do to her?"

"Extreme shortness of breath, fatigue. She'll finally have a hemorrhage or an infection she can't shake off."

"Like AIDS, you mean?"

"Something like that, yes."

Russell paused halfway through his Windsor knot. "It should have been me," he said.

HALFWAY UP HIS DRIVEWAY, Russell stopped at the edge of the woods and rolled down the car window. He looked at the frozen pond, the low, flat, irregularly-shaped arena broken by the battered remnants of cattails. He could almost hear the peepers he had counted on year after year to announce spring at the first trace of a thaw. He imagined the tentative chirp that would rise in the first weeks of April to a chorus so volante and ethereal it always seemed to float him above his mattress each night as he lay waiting for sleep, powerful enough to support the stars in their remote heights. He imagined the last traces of snow in the gullies at the edge of the woods, like the final patches of blank canvas waiting to be painted in by the spring. He saw in an instant the flowering and the paling of the fields, the gold-green darkening in July before withering under the August sun, periwinkle and chicory giving way to hawkweed and purple vetch and snow again. He saw them not as separate seasons but as a continual evolution of a single thing. He smelled lilacs and sweet basil and mockorange, though in the air around him there was only the chilling astringency of ice.

He tried to imagine the doomed girl and everything she might have wanted from life and wouldn't have. We can't take on so much as a fart for someone else, he thought. He remembered the anguish Buck Leach had suffered with the impending failure of his insurance company and his imminent bankruptcy—the restlessness, the brave face, the dread of his fall from grace as a successful businessman, how he had tried to comfort Buck with the philosophical verities of "viewing it from a larger perspective," while at the same time harboring a furtive satisfaction that it was Buck's bankruptcy they were discussing and not his own. He remembered the lion cubs he and Miriam had watched at play on the photo safari they had taken in Kenya, how kittenlike they were, as innocent of the life of killing to which they had been born as the children of Tapua.

In his sleep that night he stood on the dock on a perfect day in June. "A transparent summer morning" was the phrase that came to mind. He breathed in the sky and the reflection of one small white cloud in the black mirror of the water, and then he was falling backwards, and the sky disappeared. He was being pulled into the dark, and that was all. It was peaceful there, with no thought of any other place or of time passing.

42

BECAUSE THE THOUGHT SEEMED VENAL, Lesley tried not to acknowledge it. At first she was hurt and then angry. Russell's short good-bye note struck her as patronizing as she reflected on it. Goddamn him, she thought, how could he think I could be so naive? It pleased her to feel the injured party. But after the anger and the initial wave of sorrow, she was left with a solution, a burden dissolved.

She wondered if he had suspected her feelings for Tom. A presence had come between them, a stifling politeness. Finally, she hadn't wanted Russell as a lover, yet she couldn't bear the thought of losing him altogether. Sometimes she felt him as an abiding presence, felt she might turn and see him, quiet and wise and unassuming. She wanted to believe she would never have thrown him over for Tom, but she couldn't be sure, and she was haunted by the suspicion that Russell had tired of her.

With Tom she found an excitement she hadn't known even in the beginning with Nick, a bloodsport need and an intensity of attachment she had felt only for Katy. She felt anxious whenever she thought of him and wished a person could have two lives. Before Tom, she had been comfortable with Russell, and that might have been enough. It occurred to her that, without Russell in the interim, she might have found Tom too threatening.

But comfort wasn't enough. On Christmas night it became clear to Lesley that she had become a prisoner of her compassion, or her idea of compassion, and that the gratitude she felt toward Russell could only turn to resentment. After eating a light supper and seeing Katy to bed, Russell had suggested they make love. But for Leslie it was music that had become too predictable, and she begged off with a headache. She had been thinking about Tom, returning alone to his empty apartment after having dinner with Taylor Stanley and his family, and she wanted to be there with him.

Marlis called to tell her that she had been contacted by Grant Gresham, Russell's attorney, who said that Russell had left a power of attorney instructing him to disburse his property. Half of it was intended for an Indian education fund in South Dakota, $200,000 went to Josephine and the remaining five million or so worth of Wheeler stock was to be divided equally between Nick, Marlis, Lesley and Katy. Lily had come to live with them two weeks earlier when Josephine had found the brief note assuring her that her retirement had been provided for and asking her to take Lily to Lesley's house.

Tom, who was a director of the Bank of Five Oaks, learned that Russell had cashed out an even half-million in money market funds and transferred them to the Westmac Bank of Australia. "Australia's a big place," he pointed out. "Nobody's likely to find Russell if he doesn't want to be found."

Lesley felt Lily's jowls come to rest on her knee as she sat at the kitchen table with the checkbook open, ready to deal with the post-Christmas bills. She took a moment to sort through the day's mail, and she noticed the unusual stamp, the postmark—Brisbane, Queensland—and the address in Russell's unmistakable Palmer-method hand. She held the letter a moment and noticed how it quivered between her fingers. She turned it over, slit the envelope along the flap with a table knife and unfolded a single page of hotel stationery.

Dear Lesley, I'm sorry I didn't say good-bye, but you would've pleaded with me to stay, and there would've been last looks and tears, and we might've said things we'd wish we hadn't.

I took a walk on the beach this morning and looked out

east toward the Coral Sea, over seven thousand miles of water in which nothing we worry about is any more significant than one krill or microscopic piece of plankton. It was a nude beach. In fact I think all the beaches here are potentially nude beaches. The Australians seem pretty indifferent about such things. I think I was the only one actively looking at those bodies so beautifully open to the air.

Brisbane isn't anything like I remember it from the war. It's a big city. I only remember barracks and a sort of a ramshackle place, but I had my mind on other things then.

There's nothing to be sad about. We all grow old and die, if we're lucky. If I'd stayed I'd only have spoiled your memories. You need to find someone you can grow old with. This way you can remember me at my best, or near-best, not as some bad-smelling set of symptoms. I was just getting bored. I need an adventure.

How stupid, Lesley thought. How melodramatic and unworthy. But then her attitude softened.

I appreciate your taking care of Lily. You're the only one I know who will give her the attention she needs. You gave me what I needed, and I appreciate it deeply. I've had more than anyone should expect out of life.

Last night I woke up in a sweat and thought about you and what you might be doing in the middle of the afternoon in Five Oaks. I had lots of thoughts like that during the war, but they passed. And now it doesn't seem like such a big deal, anymore than letting go of what I did yesterday or the dream I had this morning. Tomorrow I'm going to a beautiful place, and it's right here on earth.

I wouldn't have minded a little more time with you and Katy. I wish I could've been the right man for you; I wish Nick could've been. But you and I both know that what we think we want doesn't make any difference in the end, and to paraphrase our friend, who am I that this world has disappointed me?

I love you,
Russ

43

He kicked open the cargo door and felt the blast of the wind and the propwash. He checked the cinch of his parachute and the static-lines to the crates on the conveyor track. Then he braced himself in the bay and looked down at the once familiar green land, the dark river winding through the gorge, the transparent summer morning. He inhaled deeply and was sure he could smell it; the damp, slightly metallic odor of the forest, like leaves underfoot after a rain in October. It was mid-morning, and there were no signs yet of the clouds the afternoon would bring with their monsoon-like rains. He took another deep breath. Who am I, he thought, that this world has disappointed me?